"So are you saying that what we had wasn't real?"

"I didn't say that."

"Then what are you saying? Look at me, Danica."

Jaden reached up and cupped her chin and pinned her with his penetrating gaze, holding her so she couldn't look away. She swallowed, stared into his hot, sable-brown eyes and fought not to tremble. She knew that determined look. She had seen it many times before, usually when he wanted something badly.

"You can't tell me that what we had wasn't real. I felt it and I know that you felt it, too. And as much as you might want to deny it, it's still alive and kicking between us. Come here." Before she realized what he was doing, he'd put their food on the backseat and pulled her across the seat and onto his lap, where she felt his heart pounding heavily. "Feel that? That's what you do to me."

Books by Angie Daniels

Kimani Romance

The Second Time Around
The Playboy's Proposition
The Player's Proposal

ANGIE DANIELS

is an award-winning author of twelve works of romance and fiction. A chronic daydreamer, she knew early on that someday she wanted to create page-turning stories of love and adventure. Born in Chicago, Angie has spent the past twenty years residing in and around Missouri, and considers the state her home. Angie holds a master's in human resource management. For more on this author you can visit her Web site at www.angiedaniels.com.

The player's proposal

angie daniels

KIMANI™ ROMANCE

This book is dedicated to Princess. Thanks for holding it
down while I was trying to do my thang. Luv ya

 KIMANI PRESS™

ISBN-13: 978-0-373-86090-6
ISBN-10:   0-373-86090-0

THE PLAYER'S PROPOSAL

Copyright © 2008 by Angie Daniels

www.kimanipress.com

Printed in U.S.A.

Dear Reader,

Welcome back to Sheraton Beach, Delaware, where the people are friendly, the beaches fabulous and love is always in the air!

I want to thank all of you for your kind e-mails telling me how much you love those fine Beaumont brothers, Jabarie and Jaden. Now it brings me great pleasure to give you Jaden and Danica.

After a disagreement, Jaden is the last man Danica wants to see, but when her car breaks down she has no choice but to ask for his help. Jaden's more than willing to help as long as she agrees to his proposal. Ooh-wee! It's about to get hot in here!

Writing this book was another pleasurable experience. So sit back and get ready for another trip to the coast.

Enjoy!

Angie Daniels

Prologue

Danica Dansforth snuggled deeper into the covers and released a heavy sigh. *I'm in love!*

A smile played on her lips at the memories. Last night had been everything she could ever have hoped for and then some. The caressing. The kissing. The two of them coming together as one. How was she to have known that the day she met Jaden Joshua Beaumont, her entire world would change? No one had warned her of the power of sexual attraction or the possibility of lust turning into love.

Danica felt the soreness between her legs, but she wasn't complaining, instead she released a deep satisfying breath. Jaden Beaumont knew how to make a female feel how a woman should feel—loved and completely satisfied. Her smile deepened. How many times had they made love last night? Three? Four? With

Jaden, she could stay in bed and make love for the next year and it still wouldn't be nearly enough.

With her face buried in a pillow, Danica allowed her mind to travel back to four weeks ago, when her friend Sheyna Simmons suggested they meet for lunch at Spanky's Bar and Grill. The moment she stepped through the door and walked toward Sheyna's table, Danica found herself face-to-face with the finest man she had met in a long time. She'd never forget Jaden rising from his chair. Six-four with the sinewy physique of a bodybuilder, he towered over her. All Danica could do was stare up into deep sable-brown eyes that had had the power to make her come undone with a single glance.

Danica rolled over only to find the spot beside her on the bed empty. Opening her eyes, she blinked and adjusted to the bright sun beaming through the vertical blinds in Jaden's bedroom. Outside, the Pacific Ocean loomed on the horizon and a white sandy beach filled her view. She had only been in California a short time, yet she was already considering relocating so she could be closer to the man she loved.

Rising from the bed, she reached for the burgundy sateen sheet and wrapped it snugly around her body, then padded down the hallway of the condominium in search of Jaden. Hearing his deep baritone voice, she moved toward the kitchen and was just about to enter when she realized he was on the phone.

"Who's the man, Jace? Who's the man! Didn't I tell you I would have that redhead eating out of the palm of my hand? She loves me. You hear me? I had her begging for my attention! *Ha-ha!* As soon as I stepped through the door, she was all over me…whatever, man. She's a sad little puppy when I'm not around…you need to start listening to your baby brother. I know what it takes to win over the ladies." He paused and laughed again. "Cash only, big brother, because that's the easiest five hundred dollars I've ever won."

Mortified, Danica stared at his back. Her mouth opened but no words came out. Finally, she turned on her heels and stumbled back down the hall. It had all been some kind of joke that he was now bragging about! Jaden had bet his brother five hundred dollars that he would have her eating out of the palm of his hand. Her stomach ached and she fought back tears as she returned to the bedroom. From down the hall, she could still hear Jaden's laughter and anger boiled up inside her. How dare he make fun of her!

Storming over to the closet, she removed her suitcase and quickly started filling it with her things. She tossed her shoes in, then moved over to his dresser and pulled out the few items she had brought for her trip. With every chuckle coming from the other room, hurt and humiliation washed over her.

Last night Jaden told her he loved her. The confession had brought tears to her eyes and Danica could barely speak when she told him she loved him, as well. It had all been one big joke. Well, he would regret ever messing with her.

Pushing her shoulder-length auburn hair away from her face, Danica reached for her cell phone and called the airport with every intention of being on the first plane back to Sheraton Beach, Delaware. As far as Danica was concerned, their relationship was officially over.

Chapter 1

Eighteen months later

Standing in front of Peterson's Garage was the last place in the world Danica wanted to be. Unfortunately, she didn't have much of a choice. She sighed deeply and rubbed her forehead. Living in a small beachfront town with only one auto body shop, she had limited options unless of course she wanted her car towed to the next town, which was more than thirty miles away.

Danica groaned inwardly and clenched and un-clenched her fingers around the strap of her expensive leather handbag. If she had the extra cash, she wouldn't have hesitated in paying the additional charge. Anything to keep her from having to find herself face-to-face with the one man she'd rather avoid.

Jaden Joshua Beaumont.

"Miss, would you like for me to wait?"

She glanced over her shoulder at the cab driver. Her grim expression softened as she swung around to stare into warm brown eyes that reflected kindness and concern. For a moment, she had forgotten he was still there, waiting patiently for instruction. Danica shook her head, then with trembling fingers reached inside her purse and removed a crisp ten-dollar bill. "No, I can walk back," she replied with a hint of despair. After handing him the fare, she stood at the curb and watched the cab leave, trying to prolong the inevitable as long as possible. But the moment of reckoning had finally arrived.

Almost exactly a year ago, Jaden had sold his body shop in California and returned to Sheraton Beach, Delaware, to take over Mr. Peterson's Garage. Since then, Danica had done everything in her power to avoid him. She stopped going to her favorite restaurant on Fridays, grocery shopped at odd hours of the day, and utilized drive-through windows, anything not to risk running into Jaden. Danica had been successful at avoiding him for almost twelve months, but her luck had finally run out.

Although she had prepared for this moment from the second AAA informed her that her car had been towed to Peterson's Garage, she still wasn't ready to face Jaden again. Unfortunately, there was nothing she could do but get prepared. All her reasons for avoiding Jaden had finally come to an end. With one final breath, Danica turned on the heels of her espadrilles and headed toward the door.

As she stepped into the building, the air-condition-ing hit her with a rush she welcomed. She was already perspiring in her dress, but this didn't have anything to do with the seventy degree temperatures outside.

"Hi, can I help you?" the girl behind the desk asked as she ended a phone call.

Danica stared into the face of a young woman whose lips curved into a generous smile. "Umm…" Danica began, then paused long enough to clear her throat. "My Mercedes was towed in here about an hour ago."

Her green eyes lit up knowingly. "Oh, yes, the vintage one! She's a beauty! Go on back. He's looking at her right now." She pointed toward the garage behind the floor-to-ceiling glass window.

"Thank you."

As Danica moved through the door the knot in her stomach tightened even more. With wobbly legs, she walked across the large garage toward her car, heart pounding in her throat. Any second now and she'd find herself—

"Have you ever heard of motor oil?"

The baritone voice startled her. No hello or how are you doing? Just straight and to the point.

"Wh-what did you say?" she stuttered, his smooth, seductive sound still echoing in her ear. Danica moved closer to her Mercedes just as a man rolled the creeper out from beneath the car. And there he was standing before her, the man she had once loved with all her heart.

Jaden Beaumont.

Suddenly her breath caught, her skin prickled, and every nerve in her body went taut when her gaze collided with his. Streaks of motor oil and grease covered his navy-blue uniform and yet Jaden still managed to look powerful and sleek. He seemed stronger, more potent than before and memories of their explosive relationship began tumbling through her mind.

She took a quick sweep of his tall, athletic body, returning to his milk-chocolate face. Long dark locks rested comfortably at his shoulders. Swallowing, she remembered so many nights of grabbing hold of his hair and holding on while he was buried deep inside her. Those beautiful sable-brown eyes were watching her, and desire tore through Danica when he finally spoke again. This time his voice was deep and slow like that of a sleepy lover.

"When was the last time you had an oil change?"

Snapping out of the trance, Danica shook her head and pressed her lips tightly together as she pondered his question. Since retiring from modeling, she had moved into the house her grandmother Ujema Jacobs had left in her will, and had been working nonstop from sunup to sundown to open her boutique. Buying groceries and changing oil had been the furthest things from her mind. In fact, she was too embarrassed to admit that twice she found herself on the side of the road because she had forgotten to get gas.

"What does that have to do with anything?" she replied, not at all liking the scolding look he was giving her.

"It means your engine has locked up," he replied, the words clattering out in a growl.

Not understanding, Danica simply shrugged. "Okay, so add some oil and fix it. I'm sure…"

Jaden cut her off with a shake of his head and a harsh laugh. "It's not quite that simple."

She swallowed once, then licked her lips. "What do you mean?"

Reaching for a rag, Jaden wiped his hands off as he spoke. "It means that you'll need a new engine."

"A new engine?" she repeated with a pang of

panic. "You're kidding, right?" But even as she said it Danica knew Jaden would never joke about something that serious.

"No," he replied.

She slammed her eyelids shut and took a deep breath before opening them again. "Okay…so how much will it cost to fix it?"

He tossed the towel aside and glanced at her. "About five grand."

"Five grand!" she gasped. "Why so much?"

"Because that's how much it will cost to replace the engine of a classic 1965 Mercedes Pagoda. You want to drive luxury? Well, it doesn't come cheap."

The purse strap slipped from her shoulder, which now drooped with despair. There was no way she could come up with that much money. "I can't afford it."

Jaden's gaze came up, his curiosity drawing his thick brows together. "All the money you've earned modeling…why not?"

Under the slash of those arrogant sable eyes, she wanted to cut him down to size, but he was right. After working ten years as a model, she had earned a hefty nest egg. Last year, all she had to do was reach inside her purse and write a check without a blink of the eye. But that was before her accountant extorted funds, stealing thousands of dollars of her money. Even though he was now serving seven to ten years in prison, she would never get her money back. What little she'd had left, Danica had poured into her business, Ujema Swimwear, named after her grandmother. Until she turned a profit, money was going to be tight. "Everything I have is tied into my business."

Jaden stared at her for a long time before he replied

with a shrug, "Then you'll probably be better off trading in the Mercedes and buying a cheaper, more affordable car."

"I can't do that! That car belonged…to my father. It's all I have left of him." Her voice faltered slightly and she hated that he witnessed a weak moment. Jaden gave her a puzzled look, and she took a deep breath and answered the question burning in his eyes. "My father passed away eight months ago." She suddenly felt like crying. It hadn't been nearly enough time to grieve.

Danica noticed the second the news hit Jaden because his eyes softened. "I'm sorry." She watched as he struggled for something else to say but instead looked at her with mute sympathy. "He was a nice man."

"Thank you." His comment meant a great deal to her. The two had never gotten a chance to meet, yet spoken on the phone on several occasions.

Danica took a deep breath. David Dansforth had meant the world to her, and only days after spending Fourth of July weekend together, the firefighter had died saving an elderly woman and her cat from a burning building. When her father hadn't been putting out fires, he had been at home tinkering with his car. That Mercedes had been his pride and joy.

Just like his baby girl.

There was a long silence. That dark gaze roamed over her face and lowered to her mouth and she felt her lips tingle. Without thinking, she licked her bottom lip. Dammit, Jaden was studying her the way a man studied a woman. Feeling the intensity of his gaze, she struggled to keep her emotions in check. Her nipples tightened, while warmth pooled between her legs. His face was barely an inch from hers and she knew if she leaned the slightest bit toward him, she'd risk her sanity to experience just one more kiss.

This is definitely getting out of hand.

Danica quickly turned her head, not wanting Jaden to see what she was feeling inside.

"I think I could possibly rebuild it for half that price, but it's still going to cost you," she heard him reply after a long silence. Then without bothering to explain the conditions of his statement, Jaden walked away and headed toward a small office at the back of the garage. When it became obvious he wasn't returning, Danica followed his steps and found him standing behind a cluttered desk.

"What's it going to cost me?" she asked impatiently. Reaching up, she pushed away loose strands of hair and wished she had put it in a ponytail.

"I need a receptionist," he finally said.

"Receptionist?" she gasped. "Me?" *No way.* "What's wrong with the girl at the desk?"

Jaden snorted rudely, then returned his gaze to her. "She's a college student who's been helping me during the school year, but finals are next week. Not to mention she plans to travel around Europe this summer."

Danica looked down at the mess cluttering his desk as she desperately searched for another excuse. "Then why don't you just run an ad in the newspaper and hire someone?"

"I did that but I've been so busy I haven't had a chance to review the résumés or schedule interviews. That's where you would come in."

Uh-uh. The last thing she needed was to be sharing space and air with him for any long periods of time. Memories of their last night together came to mind when they were sharing a lot more than just air. She swallowed hard against the knot of emotions settling at her gut that she hadn't felt in months. "I don't think that's a good idea."

"Why not?" There was a slight roughness to his voice.

Danica pressed her lips together. That would be too damn close for comfort. The farther away from Jaden she was, the better off they'd both be. "We both know why not," she managed around a breath.

Jaden gave her a pointed look. "Yes, I guess we do. The *fiancé* you never bothered to tell me about. By the way, how is he doing?" His mouth curved slightly while one thick dark eyebrow lifted, challenging her.

Danica groaned inwardly. She should have known he'd bring up the reason why she had ended their relationship. Or at least the excuse she'd given him. She didn't want to go where he was leading. At this point, there was really no reason to bring up the past. "He's fine."

Jaden's mouth twitched. "Glad to hear it," he said in a tone that took on a hint of bitterness, which irritated her.

What was his problem? she wondered with a frown. If anyone had a right to be angry, it should be her. She was the one who had gotten hurt back then, not him. But instead of a retort, she decided to let the comment slide.

He reached down for a sheet of paper in front of him, then glanced up at her, eyes narrowed, mocking her. "Well, do you want the job or not?" His voice grated her senses. They both knew she was at a disadvantage and not in a position to refuse his offer, yet that didn't stop her from trying.

Inhaling deeply, she tried convincing Jaden why it

wasn't a good idea. "I have a boutique to open. There is no way I can be in two places at the same time."

"Mornings will be fine," he replied. With his gaze zeroed in on her face, he moved around the desk and towered over her.

Danica ran her fingers through her hair and cleared her throat, trying to give herself time to organize her thoughts. When she started to decline, Jaden held up a hand and said impatiently, "The clock is ticking, so I'm going to ask you again. You want my help or not?"

While waiting for an answer, Jaden watched Danica nibble nervously on her bottom lip the way he remembered her doing any time she was seriously considering something. While she thought about his offer, he tried to dismiss the sensation prowling over his body as he took in every single luscious curve.

He stared into her beautiful amber eyes that even after more than a year he still couldn't get out of his mind. Danica Dansforth was beautiful and her face was so familiar to him. Not because she once graced the covers of almost every fashion magazine on the stand. Nope. It was because even after eighteen months, he still dreamed about her on nights when his mind gave him no peace. Who could forget those high cheekbones, small protruding nose and long reddish-brown hair? Even now he had to squeeze his hand in a fist to keep from touching her delectable skin that reminded him of sweet cashews. Natural arching eyebrows set off eyes that were taunting and veiled by her sweeping eyelashes. His gaze shifted to her full painted lips. Jaden vividly remembered their first kiss, and her delicious taste as his tongue explored her mouth. A shiver of desire tore through him. He was glad that he was wearing loose-fitting pants, blocking a view of an apparent arousal straining against his boxers. Lust surged inside him, which further frustrated him. He didn't want to want her.

But I'm a man.

And a man knows a beautiful woman when he sees one.

Jaden dragged his eyes from her lips and did another slow sweep of her body. The floral-print wrap dress that tied at the waist was feminine and downright sexy. He lingered at her long, gorgeous legs that ended in heaven, he remembered all too well, draped around his waist. All six sleek feet of her aroused him since the second he spotted her walking across the restaurant. When she had turned his way and smiled, he'd been a goner. Never before had he been so aroused, so immediately attracted. Desire had ricocheted through his body and held him hostage. Even now he had to swallow to get his bearings when he felt his body responding to just being near her for the first time in almost eighteen months.

A heavy groan escaped his lips as he concluded that even though Danica had given up modeling, she was more beautiful than ever before. She had added a few attractive pounds to her statuesque frame. Her face was fuller, more radiant, and her hips more generous and sexier than ever. Even now he could allow himself to get lost in her looks.

Been there.

Done that.

And all he had gotten in return was games.

To this day, he remembered Danica telling him the morning after an insatiable night, a night when he had confessed his love, that she had enjoyed their time together, but it was time to return to her life and to a fiancé Danica had never even bothered to mention. It had been a hard pill to swallow. The woman he had planned to spend the rest of his life with hadn't really loved him at all.

At seeing her again, his reaction proved that he hadn't quite gotten her out of his system. Already he could feel her body's warmth, the sensation clouding his decision to stay clear of her.

Damn her!

Even now he had a strong urge to tug her into his arms and hold her against him. Watching her standing there, wide-eyed, with her lips parted, he felt his unsteady emotions. He resented the woman in front of him, all curves and softness. Danica was a predator waiting to take her next victim. Not him. He had learned a hard lesson. Exasperated, he gave up waiting.

"Danica, what's it going to be?"

She reached up to push back loose strands of hair, then spoke each word as if she had carefully given them some thought. "No, I don't think that's a good idea."

Something within made him push on, when any other man would have just shrugged and left well enough alone. He wasn't any man. He wasn't even sure why he insisted. Maybe because, despite her bravado, Danica looked as if she was desperate for help. Or maybe it was simply his stubborn pride. "All I ask is for a couple of weeks. Long enough to help me get my business files in order and identify a candidate. In exchange, I'll replace your engine…free of charge."

Danica straightened. "Free?"

Nodding, Jaden didn't know where that idea came from other than he knew the generous offer would get her attention. Sure enough, he could see her mind working and tried to read her expression. He figured she wanted so desperately to preserve her father's car that she was seriously giving his offer consideration.

Moving around his desk, Jaden lowered into the chair, then shifted forward in his seat and reached for a folder and started flipping through its contents. Mostly auto parts he needed to call and order for Monday. Even while he studied the list he could feel the wheels in Danica's brain churning. From his chair, he could smell her, that floral scent that reached inside his senses, tormenting him even further. He was a fool to even consider having her invading his space. Day after day. He could easily get a temp or run an ad for a stay-at-home mom who was looking to earn some extra money while the kids were at school. Yet as much as he knew the danger of being around her, he couldn't find the words to tell Danica to find another mechanic. Or better yet, offer to tow her car to the next town.

He watched her yawn, standing in front of his desk, then arch sensually, causing her full breasts to press against the thin material. He inhaled sharply, surprised at the sensation stirring in his chest. He found his palms itching, and he curled his fingers into them. He would have liked nothing better than to take her into the room in back, toss her down on the bed and make love to her, but what would that solve? Afterward, he would still know he couldn't trust her.

Jaden groaned inwardly at his runaway thoughts. He had completely lost his mind. He knew the dangers of playing with Danica. The effect she had on him. Once should have been enough.

"Okay, I'll do it," she finally said, smoothing her hands over her hips.

He raised his gaze to meet hers and nodded, more pleased than he should have been. He hated himself for that weakness, but with her looking at him with those soulful eyes, he felt like a bully. He wished he could get past his anger and remember why he used to love her, but he couldn't. At least not yet. "Good, then I'll see you Monday morning."

Danica nodded weakly as if admitting defeat. And for the first time he noticed the fatigue shadowing her eyes. "Okay, I'll be here," she said softly, and he heard the despair in her voice.

"Then I guess we've got ourselves a deal." He held out his hand and watched as she hesitated before accepting it. As soon as her hand touched his, Jaden could swear he felt heat travel up his arm. Danica must have felt it too, because she jerked away as if she had just been burned and turned on her heels.

Jaden watched her leave, and knew then that he was in trouble. Instead of anger, he felt his heart pounding with excitement at seeing her again on Monday.

The crazy thought sent him immediately back to work.

Chapter 2

Danica had barely made it to the boardwalk when angry tears started to surface. The look in Jaden's eyes was as clear as the blue sky above. He never really loved her at all. What a fool she had been to believe he had.

Because he told me so.

She took a deep breath of the crisp, salty air and refused to waste another tear on that irritating man. Back then, Jaden had told her a lot of things and all had been lies except for one—his dream of someday owning Peterson's Garage. Many nights she used to lie in his arms as they shared their thoughts and dreams. Owning the shop was something Jaden had confessed to wanting ever since he was eleven when the widower had first taken him under his wing and showed him how to change a flat tire. Despite everything that had happened between them, Danica was happy to see his dream finally come true.

Anxious to get away from the crowd of people, she moved to an opening on the path and took the stairs down toward the sandy beach. Her boutique was at the far end of the boardwalk. Cutting across the beach would slice her travel time in half. She reached the beach where the swell of the Atlantic Ocean caressed the shoreline, and released a sigh, glad for a few moments to clear her head.

The boardwalk was filled with shops from local merchants and offered vinegar fries, cotton candy and funnel cakes. At the far south was an amusement park that didn't open until dusk. At night the strip lit up splendidly with green, yellow and pink neon lights and flashing signs, giving the feel of the Las Vegas Strip. In a little over a month, tourists would begin fishing, swimming, sailing and visiting the dozens of shops that lined the big pier.

Excitement bubbled at her chest. She was eager to open her boutique, so visitors to Sheraton Beach could see everything she had to offer. Danica frowned. Now that her mornings were going to be spent at the garage, her availability would be cut in half. *Hmmph!* There was no way she was delaying her grand opening, she thought with a stubborn tilt of her chin. Her boutique would open on Memorial Day weekend as scheduled even if she had to invest her nights and weekends, as well.

Damn him!

This was Jaden's way of getting back at her. She was sure of it. Obviously, his ego hadn't gotten over her ending their relationship. She felt a surge of anger. Too bad. It was his fault she lied the way she had. She had been all set to spend the rest of her life with him before she had heard him bragging over the phone.

The memories of his laughter that morning still managed to make her skin crawl. She had returned to the bedroom, called the airport and showered. By the time Jaden came back to the bedroom carrying breakfast on a tray, she had been dressed and her bags packed. It took everything she had to ignore the beautiful assortment of pastries while she made up a story about being engaged. She had forced a laugh and thanked him for the month-long fling, then made it clear her heart belonged to another man. Angrily, Jaden stood back and watched as she grabbed her things and left to catch the first plane back to Delaware.

Danica briefly closed her eyes, willing the painful memories away. Yet she couldn't forget the hurt on his face. *But what about my pain?* That afternoon it had taken everything Danica had to hold it together until her cab had arrived. She'd loved Jaden from the bottom of her heart. His kisses, his mere presence had excited her. She remembered him lying beside her with that slumberous, sensual look as his eyes took in every curve of her body. She had once thought him to be the kindest, gentlest man she had ever known and after four weeks, believed him to be her soul mate, and thought they had a chance at a future together. The happiest moment of her life had been on their last night when she'd heard those four words that caused her heart to swell beneath her breasts. *I love you, Danica.* Jaden then held her tightly in his arms, making her feel as if she was the luckiest woman in the world. To her embarrassment, the next day she found out it had all been one big lie.

By the time Danica reached the boutique, she was starting to think she had lost her mind for agreeing to work at the garage. But what choice did she have? Since Oliver had wiped out her savings, she barely had enough money to stay afloat until her boutique opened. She took a deep breath, held it, then slowly let it out. Everything was going to be all right. All she had to do was work with Jaden long enough to find him a receptionist. What was difficult about that? She already knew the answer to that. Being around Jaden would only remind her of the time they once had shared. All thirty-three heart-thumping days.

Strolling into the building, she pushed the door closed with a slam putting an end to her foolish thoughts. The worst thing she could do was start thinking about that time. She had already wasted hours of unnecessary tears on a man who clearly was not worth it.

"Hey, how'd it go?" her efficient assistant asked.

"Not good," Danica replied with a huff as she flopped down into a folding chair near a large storefront window. "I'm looking at almost five grand in repairs because I didn't do something as simple as change the oil." How could she have been so sidetracked that she hadn't even noticed? Damn her oil-indicator light! Obviously it wasn't working, either.

"Five thousand dollars! Goodness! What are you going to do?" Nyree asked. Her large hazel eyes narrowed with growing concern.

She turned her gaze to the fifty-three-year-old grandmother and had to bite her lip to keep the bitterness from her voice. "We came up with an agreement."

Her thick eyebrows shifted slightly. "What kind of agreement?"

"He's without a receptionist. I agreed to work for him in the mornings, and in exchange, he's rebuilding my engine for free."

"You're kidding! Old man Peterson agreed to something like that?" Nyree asked, disbelief was apparent in her eyes.

Oh, boy. She obviously didn't know he'd retired. Danica shook her head. "Where have you been? Mr. Peterson sold the garage almost a year ago to Jaden Beaumont."

Nyree stumbled to her feet. "Jaden…Jaden Beaumont is back in town?"

"Yes, he is." Danica noticed her voice had dropped an octave, quivering slightly as if she were out of breath.

Her assistant started waving her hands frantically in the air. "Oh, my goodness! I missed that piece of gossip. Wait until I tell Carly and Josie!"

"You know him?" She hated the feeling of jealousy.

Nyree laughed, the soft sound of her voice carrying easily across the boutique. "Danica, you've got a lot to learn," she began. "In a town this size everybody knows everybody and everybody knows the Beaumonts. *Especially* Jaden."

Danica nodded. Even during summer vacations when she used to come up from Richmond to stay with her grandmother, she remembered Nana singing the family praises. The Beaumont Hotel perched on top of the hill provided employment for almost twenty-five percent of Sheraton Beach's labor market. In addition they held annual fund-raisers to support local charities. The Beaumont heirs, Jace, Jabarie and their baby sister, Bianca, ran the Beaumont Corporation, while Jaden, the black sheep of the family, chose to find his own way.

Curiosity got the better of her and Danica heard herself asking, "What do you mean *especially* Jaden?"

"Chile, Jaden has a way with the women. I heard he can talk the panties off any woman he wants. I always thought he was the cutest of the three boys with those long sexy locks," Nyree added with a dreamy smile.

Don't I know it? Even now Danica couldn't help remembering them brushing across her breasts as his mouth traveled down past her belly button to her—

She shook the thought away.

"Hell, if I wasn't old enough to be his mama, he wouldn't have to worry about talking my panties off because I would just hand them to him," Nyree chuckled.

Danica joined in on the laughter even though she knew what Nyree said was true. It wasn't until she had lived in Sheraton Beach for several months that she heard the story of the Beaumont brothers. All three were sexy as hell. Tall, gorgeous, chocolate bodies. Killer smiles. Bedroom eyes. The oldest, Jace, once had a reputation of love 'em and leave 'em before his wife showed him she was the only one he would ever need. Jabarie was the most compassionate of the three and after a second chance at getting it right with his childhood girlfriend he fought tooth and nail to make that happen. The couple were now the proud parents of one-year-old Arianna Danielle Beaumont. Jaden, the baby boy, was said to be a master at providing pleasure without promising forever. Well, Danica knew that firsthand, she thought with a scowl, because he was also the same man who had broken her heart.

She rose and moved over to the far side of the room to begin assembling a display case. "Anyway, he wants me to help him find a receptionist while covering the front desk in the morning. I don't know how I'm going to get the boutique together if I'm working over there with him."

Nyree gave her a dismissive wave. "Easy, I'll come in during the day and I'll let you handle the afternoon."

"Oh, but don't you have water aerobics in the morning?"

The older woman shook her head, smiling. "I think I can miss a couple of sessions while you help Jaden out."

"Oh, I couldn't ask you to do that."

"You're not. I'm offering," she insisted, then gave Danica a long thoughtful look. "You need your car fixed. Besides, I think the two of you make a gorgeous couple."

Danica Dansforth lifted her gaze from the case to stare at the petite woman standing to her right and laughed shortly at her comment. "I don't think so." She would work with him because she didn't have much of a choice. However, their relationship was going to be strictly business. Never again would she trust her heart to Jaden Beaumont.

Jaden slammed the hood down on a Dodge Neon and reached for a paper towel. He was so distracted he couldn't even change a couple of sparkplugs correctly.

Several hours had passed and he still couldn't believe he had asked Danica to work at the shop with him for the next couple of weeks. He must be losing it. Not after the way she had crushed his heart like an empty beer can and tossed it away in the recycling bin.

With Danica he had thought that he had met his match. From the moment he met her, every hormone in his body had gone on full alert.

Jaden had known she was different from all the other women he'd dated. When she had surprised him and flown out to Los Angeles to see him he was flattered and felt like the luckiest man in the world. The next two weeks they spent the days sightseeing and holding hands along the beach and the nights with her coming apart in his arms. Their last evening together, Jaden found himself telling Danica he loved her, and then the next morning he returned to the room to find the woman he loved packing her things. When he asked what was going on, Danica told him it was time to return to reality and her fiancé that she had conveniently forgotten to tell him about.

Jaden scowled at the memory. He hadn't gone after her. He thought it best to just let it go instead of confronting her and hurting himself further.

You're too stubborn for your own good.

Leaving a question unanswered was too much like letting her win. He'd always been too competitive to allow that to happen. As far as he was concerned, the time to find out the truth had finally arrived. He wanted to know why she hadn't told him about her fiancé. Why did she tell him she loved him if the next day she was going to mention another man and then leave? And that's why he gave Ginny the next month off with pay so she could study for her finals before returning home for the summer. It wasn't a complete lie. Ginny was planning to leave anyway. He'd just speeded up the process. Now he had the excuse he needed to have Danica around long enough to get her to tell him why. And by the time Danica finished identifying a receptionist, he would have his answers. Nothing more. Maybe once he had his answers, he could finally move on and finally forget her.

"What's on your mind?"

Jaden glanced over at the door and was surprised to see his brother Jace heading his way. The brothers were equally tall at six feet four inches and athletically built, but Jace's hair was short and cropped in contrast to Jaden's shoulder-length locks.

"What do you mean what's on my mind?" he asked as he watched Jace strolling into the garage with his hands buried inside his expensive pants.

His big brother stopped and leaned a hip against the Neon. "I mean, I've been standing here for almost two minutes watching you staring off into space. What's up?"

"Nothing's up," Jaden snapped, irritated that his siblings could always tell when something was bothering him.

He took in Jace's athletic physique in a gray tailor-made suit and a pale pink shirt. His brother was definitely a man who was secure with his masculinity. Suits were something Jaden seldom if ever wore, whereas Jace had a different suit for every day of the month. It was a great example as to how different he was from his big brother. Yet despite everything, the Beaumont brothers were dominate, compassionate men with a strong family commitment.

Jaden forced a half smile. "What can I do for you?"

"I thought I'd drop by and see how you're doing with my baby."

Jaden grinned at his reference to the 1969 Mustang Jace bought from a collector, which he wanted returned to its original condition. Jaden worked on it a few hours a week when time allowed. "It's coming along," he said, trying to keep his voice nonchalant. "The carburetor arrived today. I should have it installed sometime next week."

Jace glanced over to the left of the garage, admiring his car, when his brow rose with surprise. "Isn't that Danica's Mercedes?"

Jaden swore under his breath. He should have known his brother would recognize the candy-apple-red car. He averted his gaze. "Yep. Tom towed it in this morning." Tom was the on-call tow-truck driver who helped when he needed him to pick up parts or tow in a car.

"Have you seen her yet?"

Jaden cleared his throat. "Yep."

After a thoughtful moment, Jace's lips eased into a soft grin. "And did the two of you talk?"

"Yep, about her car," he replied, deliberately being evasive.

Jace gave him a scolding look. "You know what I mean."

Yep, he knew. Jaden also knew his brother was beginning to annoy him. "It's best to leave well enough alone."

Jace was silent, gauging his reaction, while Jaden decided it was time to get back to work and reached for a wrench.

A knowing smile crinkled Jace's sable eyes. "Fine, keep fooling yourself. You still love that woman and you know it." There was a hint of laughter in his voice.

Jaden looked over at his big brother, who wore a smug look, and scowled. *I guess that's what I get for following my heart rather than my head.* First and last time. He had learned his lesson. "What Danica and I had is over. The only thing we can do now is try and be civil with each other for the next couple of weeks." The words were already out of Jaden's mouth when he realized what he had said.

He wasn't at all surprised when Jace asked, "Why the next couple of weeks?"

Clearing his throat, Jaden replied, "She's going to be helping me here in the office when Ginny goes back to school."

Jace gave him an incredulous look before he tossed his head back and started laughing. The fact that he was finding humor with the idea of the two of them working together angered Jaden.

"What the hell is so funny?" Jaden barked.

Jace stopped laughing long enough to say, "You, if you really think the two of you can go from being lovers to just friends."

Last year, Jace had traded in his player's card and married Sheyna Simmons, whom he had known most of his life, and now he thought he was an expert on love and marriage.

Maybe Jace was right. Maybe the two of them working together was a recipe for disaster. But it was going to have to work because they each needed the other's help. And as far as he was concerned, no matter how attracted he was to Danica, they could never go back to the way things were. All he cared about was getting answers. Then maybe, just maybe, he could get her out of his system once and for all, so he could finally move on with his life.

Chapter 3

Danica rose from her knees and released a heavy groan. She definitely needed to start going back to the gym. At one time she prided herself on faithfully working out four to five times a week, but since she retired from modeling, going to the gym was the last thing on her mind. Instead she poured all her time and energy into trying to see her dream come true.

She reached for her mug, then moved over to the pot and filled it to the brim with piping hot French vanilla coffee. As she took a sip, her eyes traveled to all the boxes lining the boutique and released another groan. It was going to be a long weekend.

After a night of tossing and turning, Danica finally gave up trying to sleep and climbed out of bed, grabbed a quick shower and took a walk along the beach. She carried her shoes and allowed the seaweed to move carelessly around her feet, watching the sun skimming the ocean and the seagulls soaring against the morning sky. Next thing she knew she was back at the boutique working.

Might as well, she thought with a scowl, then reached for a package of artificial sweetener and poured the entire contents into her coffee. If she was going to be working down at the garage every morning, then she was going to have to find a way to make up the time, and that meant she was going to have to pour every available second into the boutique in order to make her grand opening Memorial Day weekend. The weekend officially marked the start of the season and was usually one of the busiest times of the year, which was why she had to open on time no matter what.

Damn Jaden Beaumont!

Angrily, she put her mug down and reached for a cordless drill, then moved over to the wall and started drilling more holes. Now that the walls had all been painted tangerine, she had several shelves to install. Hopefully by the time Nyree arrived at ten, they could begin putting items up on display.

As she drilled a couple of holes, she imagined the wall was Jaden's head. Because of him she had bags beneath her eyes and because of him she had tossed and turned. Dammit, if anyone had a hole in the head was her because she had spent the entire evening thinking about him.

What's wrong with me? It had been eighteen months since their breakup, yet she couldn't stop thinking about him. The time they had spent together had been magical and unlike anything she'd ever experienced before, which was probably why she had fallen head over heels so fast. She had never been a hopeless romantic. Yet with limited experience she had truly believed the words Jaden confessed were real.

When she was modeling, she hadn't had much time for relationships and that had been fine with her because to her it was just one of those sacrifices one had to make in order to get what one wanted.

For as long as she could remember, her parents had wanted her to be a model. She was entered into baby contests at three months old and was competing at the regional level by the time she was five. After graduating from Our Lady of Peace High School, Danica signed with a modeling agency. That initial job at age eighteen launched an international modeling career that included runway shows, magazines and commercials. At twenty she secured a large cosmetics contract when she signed with Revlon. She was also among the few black models to be featured on the cover of the *Sports Illustrated* swimsuit issue. Everything she had done was for her parents. She had few friends and while growing up she never was around long enough to have a real serious relationship. When Danica's mother passed away from an aneurism when she was twenty-three, she continued to follow her mother's dream. But the long hours and living out of a suitcase started to take a toll on her emotions and her body. And long before her father was killed, Danica had sat him down and told him she was ready to live her own life. She was a simple girl from Richmond and more than ready to put down roots and live in her own home instead of hotels. To her amazement her father told her that he loved her for seeing her mother's dream come true and he would support her in any decision that she made. She blinked back tears at the memory. With her father's blessings, at twenty-six she walked away from a way of life that had become as essential to her as breathing. Other than doing a benefit fashion show in two weeks, she was finally free to live her life the way she always wanted: by her own rules.

Reaching for a long screw, she released a heavy breath. That life was now behind her. She was now a business owner. All she needed now was to meet a man so that maybe she could someday start a family.

Yeah, right.

She released a bark of laughter at the ridiculous idea. Her? Married? Most of the men she'd dated were more interested in what they saw on the outside and were just as eager to see how fast they could get her into bed. Rarely had she met a man interested in knowing what she was about. That was one thing that had attracted her to Jaden. He was interested in hearing what she had to say, and when she talked, he listened. Their time together had been about a lot more than just sex. For hours they could just hold each other and talk. His discussions about the future had always included her, or at least that's what she thought. Running a hand across her curls, Danica closed her eyes and inhaled deeply before slowly letting out her breath as she wished for the umpteenth time she could get Jaden off her mind.

Reaching for the first shelf, she positioned it on the wall and was pleased with the result. *One down, twenty-four more to go.*

When she had first decided to open a swimsuit shop, Danica had no idea opening her own business was such hard work and costly. Leasing space, insurance, payroll, not to mention supplies and merchandise to fill the store, the charges were constantly rising. Her savings account was beyond sad, which was why she had agreed to do a benefit fashion show. That money would be enough to hire another part-time salesperson.

Pushing away a feeling of despair, Danica lowered herself onto the floor and took a moment to replace the bit on the cordless drill.

"What are you doing here this early in the morning?"

Danica glanced over her shoulder when she heard the familiar voice. Her grim expression softened and a smile tilted her lips as she stared at Sheyna Simmons Beaumont standing in the door. The beautiful woman and she had been close friends since she moved to Sheraton Beach almost two years ago. Sheyna had a way of making her feel as if they had been friends for years.

Her gaze lingered on the woman with an athletic build to die for. As usual, she was dressed to impress the way only Sheyna could manage even on her day off. The lime-green short-sleeve shirt was the exact shade of her sandals. They spiced up a simple pair of jeans that show-cased her hourglass figure. Danica had never been able to pull off that shade of green with her complexion, but for Sheyna it nicely accented her deep mahogany complexion. There was an air of serenity surrounding Sheyna, which always made Danica feel at ease.

Danica lowered the drill but didn't bother to rise from the floor as she said, "I should be asking you that question. It's barely nine o'clock. What are you doing all the way on this side of town?"

Sheyna stepped into the boutique and the door closed softly behind her. "I needed a walk along the beach to clear my head. Jace has a crew working on the house and all that banging and renovation is driving me crazy! I am so tired of people being in and out of my house."

Danica gave her a sympathetic grin. On the day he proposed, Jace had surprised his wife with a beautiful farmhouse, like the one Sheyna had grown up in. Now he was doing everything he needed to make it a home for the two of them.

"How much more work do you have?"

"Too much," Sheyna groaned.

"When do you think they'll be finished?"

"Not soon enough and that's what scares me. My housewarming party is in a week, so the house has got to be finished or else I am going to strangle my husband. He's worse than a woman!" she exclaimed, although a hint of a smile tugged at the corners of her mouth. "Jace wants a certain look and wants *everything* done to his standards. Do you know he waited until the contractor installed oak cabinets before he decided he wanted cherry instead? I about flipped."

Danica's eyes shone with amusement. She wasn't buying her frustration. Sheyna was obviously getting a great deal of joy out of the renovation project. Even though the couple had been married for eleven months, they still acted like newlyweds. On several occasions, Danica had caught the two of them in heated kisses. Part of her was happy for what the couple had, but it was also a painful reminder of what her life was still lacking.

Sheyna gave a sweep of her manicured fingernails. "But enough about my house and hubby. What about you? I heard your car broke down."

Danica frowned at the friendly reminder. "Yes, and it's going to cost me more money than I can afford."

A grin covered Sheyna's face as she moved to pull up a chair and took a seat. "Yes, but according to Jace, you and Jaden have worked out some kind of deal."

Danica struggled not to blush, which was no easy task. Instead she shrugged as if it were no big deal. "I'm going to help him find a receptionist and he's going to fix my car for free."

"Free?" Her smile widened. "Jaden must still really like you."

To Sheyna's disappointment, Danica never disclaimed the details of their breakup. She had been tempted several times but she didn't want to force Sheyna to have to take sides. "Nah, we're just doing each other a favor."

Sheyna didn't look the least bit convinced. "Yeah, right. You mean to tell me you weren't excited to see Jaden again?"

"No," she lied and crossed her legs on the floor, Indian-style.

Sheyna shook her head, grinning. "I think you're lying. You've been avoiding that man for almost a year, yet every time I mention Jaden's name, your face lights up. You still like him."

Danica gave her a stern look. "Don't even go there. You already did the matchmaking and it didn't work."

Sheyna blew out a frustrated breath and replied, "You still haven't told me what happened between the two of you."

She let it go with a shrug. "Nothing worth talking about. We just decided that together was not a good fit for us."

The mahogany beauty gave her a look of disbelief. "I don't understand that. I just knew the two of you were perfect."

"I thought so, too," Danica mumbled before she realized she had said the words out loud.

"I knew it! I know it can work out. The two of you just need to talk about it."

Stubbornly, Danica shook her head. "I went through that once with a man and I refused to run after another."

Sheyna leaned back on the seat. "I'm sorry that things didn't work out between y'all. But Jaden is different, and I know that it could work out if you let it."

Danica gave a long far-off look. At one time she had believed the same things until he had broken her heart.

"I wish you would tell me what happened, so I can help you fix it." Sheyna was obviously determined to find out what happened. Some things just weren't worth fixing.

"Let's just say that our relationship was nothing but a lie and it's over. I'd rather be alone than with someone who's all about games. Besides, I'm so busy right now I really don't have time for a serious relationship."

"I didn't realize how lonely I was until I discovered how much I loved Jace. Now I couldn't imagine my life without him."

At Sheyna and Jace's wedding Danica had been entranced by the bride and groom. They were such a loving couple. What was nice was that even after a year, they were obviously still in love and happy with each other. Sighing internally, Danica realized that might never happen for her. The look in Jace's eyes as he gazed down at Sheyna during their wedding was something she kept close to her heart. She would give anything to have a man look at her the same way.

Danica's lips curled in a smile. "If you could clone your man, you could make millions. I want someone like Jace. A man who doesn't beat around the bush and is honest about what he wants. He doesn't have a problem with commitment."

Sheyna frowned as she folded her arms against her chest. "That wasn't always the case. At one point I didn't think Jace would ever let go of being single and admit how much he loved me."

Danica looked at her friend. "Yeah, but he finally did, and that is more than I can say about most men."

Sheyna gave her a long look, and Danica could tell she was trying to decipher what she was saying. "Well, don't give up on Jaden just yet. He's the baby and has always been quite stubborn. But he's no fool and eventually he'll come to his senses."

Chuckling, Danica said, "Forever the optimist."

She grinned. "I wouldn't have it any other way."

"I guess, but just keep in mind, Jaden and I are over. The best we can do is try and be friends."

Sheyna wasn't ready yet to give up. "Just give him time. Besides, from what I hear, the two of you will be working closely together for the next couple of weeks. Anything could happen," she said and wagged her eyebrows suggestively.

Danica got up from the floor and moved over to the window. "Yeah, right. I can't wait."

"At least he's easy on the eyes."

Placing her hands on her hips, Danica swung around and smiled at her friend. "Now, that I can't argue with." He was definitely eye candy.

"I think the next couple of weeks can prove to be quite interesting."

Or pure torture.

Chapter 4

On Monday, Danica rose early. While a pot of coffee brewed, she moved upstairs and down the hall to the bathroom. She lowered the stopper in the tub and turned on the faucet, then reached for a bottle of scented bubbles and poured a capful beneath the hot running water. Turning on bare feet, she moved across the hall to the master bedroom and stepped into a large walk-in closet. With her hands at her hips, she allowed her eyes to travel along the racks, looking for the perfect outfit. Today she was on a mission.

Danica planned to find something that was sexy yet conservative and make Jaden regret insisting that she work in his garage.

Last night while she'd been trying to doze off to sleep, her mind had traveled over every second of their month-long relationship. Every heart-pounding kiss.

Every late-night coast-to-coast phone call. And not once had Jaden given her any indication it was all a game. Instead he made her feel like the most desirable woman alive. Sure, he was the type of man who was used to getting his way. Hell, his cockiness was one of the reasons she agreed to go out with him in the first place. She'd always liked a man who knew what he wanted and more important, one who had no problem getting it.

She frowned because Jaden definitely had her fooled. Hook, line and sinker. She had made it too easy for him, which was probably why he'd lost interest. Well, not this time. She planned to show him exactly what he was missing.

While she weeded through her wardrobe she thought about the last date she had gone out on. Joseph Holmes. A handsome thirty-something attorney. They had a platonic relationship. A couple of times, she thought about trying to get serious but it wasn't any use. Not when she still had feelings for someone else. Turning her emotions on and off had never been easy for her. She was the type of woman that when she loved, she loved hard and as a result wore her heart on her sleeve. As a result, she'd had her heart broken one time too many.

Well, not anymore. It was time for her to turn the tables.

With a determined tilt of her chin, she reached for a double-breasted lavender suit. The short sleeve jacket and miniskirt were tasteful and sexy. Wearing a wicked smile, she padded across plush carpet and lowered the suit to the bed, then headed toward the bathroom. After today, Jaden Joshua Beaumont was going to regret letting a good thing like her go.

* * *

Jaden reached for a wrench, then slid beneath the hood of a Chrysler Sebring. Tina Graves, the owner of Tina's Collectibles, wanted to pick it up by noon. Since she promised to bring along a fresh batch of homemade peanut butter cookies, he was making her oil change his first project of the morning.

Speaking of morning, he remembered with a frown, Danica was scheduled to arrive within the next hour. He still had mixed feelings about her being here and had spent half the night tossing and turning and thinking about her. If he was lucky she wouldn't show up, especially when he had way too much work for a distraction.

Every morning, around five, he and two part-time mechanics, Kyle and Tim, arrived early in order to get a head start on clearing cars from his garage.

And that's why you need help. Danica would be in at seven when the phone would begin to ring nonstop.

He took a moment to think about what was weighing so heavily on his conscience. Conning Danica into working at the shop had been a mistake. The last thing he wanted was to spend the next several weeks up under each other. Danica might suddenly remember she had a couple of kids she had forgotten to tell him about. Just the thought caused anger to resurface. He quickly brushed the thought aside. He didn't want to waste another day thinking about her. But no matter how he felt about it, he still had a business to run and hiring her, even temporarily, was a good decision. He would just have to keep his head and maintain his distance. As far as he was concerned, the less time they spent together the better. All he wanted from Danica was answers.

Jaden again pushed his thoughts aside and finished up the oil change, then went to replace a timing belt. It wasn't long before he was so engrossed in his work that he lost track of time. He heard the bell over the front door and soon after spotted a pair of interesting purple pumps move past the car, then stop.

Jaden slid from beneath the car to find Danica standing over him in a miniskirt showing off legs that had to belong to a model. His gaze slid lower, hugging the tempting curves of her calves before landing at her feet.

As he slowly rose, he gazed at the pink blouse that hugged her heavy breasts perfectly beneath a short jacket. He diverted his eyes to her face and lingered on the smile teasing the corners of her full mouth.

"Well, I'm here. What would you like me to do?"

His breath caught as she took a deep breath, causing a gentle sway of her breasts. He wanted so badly to reach up and grab one in each—

Jaden had to clear his throat to keep from telling her what he'd really like for her to do, which involved the two of them leaned back against the hood of the car.

She wore little makeup, giving her the fresh, no-nonsense look he used to love. A jolt of desire slammed into Jaden's body. Aching to touch her, he rubbed his hands briskly along his jeans.

Someone whistled, and he suddenly remembered they weren't alone. He also discovered he wasn't the only one who noticed the tall beauty. Kyle and Tim had stopped what they were doing and were heading their way.

Danica looked over her shoulder, then turned and greeted them with a warm smile and a friendly "Hello."

Tim wiped his hands on his pants and stopped in front of her, seeming clearly intimidated by the tall beauty who towered over him by at least five inches. "Aren't you Danica Dansforth?"

She gave a nervous smile before nodding. "Yes, I am."

Tim looked over at Kyle, and their mouths dropped.

Kyle practically raced over to them, closing the distance, and gave Danica his signature gap-toothed smile. "I heard you were living here but I didn't believe it. I still have your last swimsuit edition."

She blushed. Something she always did when given unwanted attention. She had never wanted celebrity status. "Thank you."

Tim reached for a pen from his breast pocket. "Can I have your autograph?" he asked and jumped in front, blocking Kyle's view.

"Wait! I was about to ask her first!" Kyle insisted and pushed his way to the front of the line.

Jaden sighed. They were like kids with their hands in the cookie jar. It was apparent the two were determine to vie for her attention. Before things got out of hand, he figured it was time to nip the situation in the bud.

"The two of you need to get back to work." The last thing he wanted to see was the two of them tripping all over themselves. Shaking his head, Jaden stepped forward and stood with his legs parted, challenging the two to question his authority. He saw the looks of disappointment before they returned to their stations and resumed their work. He already had a strong suspicion Danica's working here would be a problem, but he never guessed it would be this kind of problem. Before they left for lunch, he was going to have a serious talk with the two and make sure they understood that Danica was here to do a job, not sign autographs. However, before he got to that he had another fish to fry.

"Follow me." He placed a hand on Danica's shoulder and steered her out of the garage. As soon as they were out of ear's range, he swung around. "Why are you dressed like that?" he asked.

"Excuse me?" She gave him an innocent look. "Like what?"

"Like that."

"What's wrong with my clothes?" she asked defensively.

"Everything."

"I like what I'm wearing."

So do I and that's the problem. "When you get oil on your fancy clothes, don't come crying to me." Frustrated at his thought, he signaled for her to follow him to the reception area. Moving behind the desk, he removed an expandable folder and a box of paper.

"Here is the appointment book. To make things easier for you I marked all available appointment times in red. The last car is four o'clock. Between phone calls I would appreciate it if you would organize these invoices by last name in this folder and then order that list of supplies thumbtacked to the board. The number to the auto parts store is on the top."

Danica swung toward him. "Got it, chief," she said, then raised her hand to her forehead and saluted him.

Her gentle floral scent drifted his way, shifting his already active libido into high gear. Quickly, he moved away, trying not to brush against her. If he touched her, he might do something crazy such as kiss her the way he'd been wanting to since he'd seen her walk across the garage in that sexy outfit. "Well, make yourself at home," he replied and was aware his voice wasn't as steady as he'd like. He then hurried off back into the garage.

As soon as Danica was alone, she giggled softly. Served him right. There was no way she could have missed the yearning in his eyes, she thought with a triumphant smirk. By the end of the day he would be eating out of the palms of her hands and begging for any scraps she was willing to toss his way.

Swinging around, she moved over to the coffeepot in the corner. Looking inside, she groaned when she discovered mold growing at the bottom of the pot. "Ugh!"

She removed the old coffee filter, then moved to the restroom at the far end and was pleased to find dishwashing liquid and a sponge at the bottom. She cleaned the pot, then filled it with fresh water, a filter and four heaping spoons of coffee and started a fresh pot.

She then busied herself straightening the waiting area. Newspapers from last week were still on the table along with something sticky. Starting to sweat, Danica removed her jacket, then retrieved the sponge and cleaned off the table. She had just turned on the television when the first customer pulled up in front of the building.

The rest of the morning breezed by along with one customer after another. She even had to make coffee again. But no matter how busy she was, Danica found herself watching Jaden through the floor-to-ceiling window. Most customers dropped their vehicles off. Others sat at the large table in the reception area and watched the work being performed on their car, looked at television or flipped through several outdated magazines. Danica was more interested in watching Jaden.

His locks were pulled back from his face and secured

with a rubber band, showing off the diamond stud he always wore in his left ear. High cheekbones blended into a lean jaw and a strong chin. Watching Jaden aroused her senses in more ways than one and she didn't like that. Breathing quietly, Danica forced herself to move away from the window, stunned by the physical need that had been dormant for months. Yet she could almost taste his wide lips brushing against hers.

Damn, what was wrong with her? How many times would Jaden have to break her heart before she finally got the hint?

Danica reached for the file folder and began alphabetizing. The phone started ringing and she welcomed the distraction. Most of the morning flew by with unlimited interruptions. The only problem was Jaden's frequent appearances into the lobby. Each time he moved through that door her pulse raced while her eyes followed him.

She was amazed at the way he greeted his customers, then explained and showed them exactly what was wrong with their car and told them how much it would cost before asking Danica to order parts. As he spoke she found herself captivated by his lips and admiring his honesty, and that bothered her. Even though she'd always known him to be nothing short of a gentleman, it was the being truthful part that angered her. As far as she was concerned, Jaden didn't know the first thing about honesty.

Danica was putting the invoices in alphabetical order when her neighbor stepped into the reception area.

"Hello, Mrs. Graves. I didn't realize your car was here."

She looked up, eyes wide with surprise. "Danica, dear, what a nice surprise. I brought it in over the weekend. What are you doing here?"

"Helping out."

She nodded with approval. "That's so nice of you. Jaden's a good guy. I'm sure he truly appreciates your help."

Not interested in discussing Jaden, Danica changed the subject. "What do you have in your hands?" she asked even though she knew the smell of her peanut butter cookies with her eyes blindfolded.

"I brought these for Jaden."

"And I smell them all the way in back." His booming voice followed him into the room and the generous smile he gave the elderly woman made Danica's heart skip a beat.

Mrs. Graves was beaming with pride as she handed him the box. He opened the lid and bit into one. As he did, he offered the cookies to Danica, and she took one, as well.

"Mmm, delicious," he said, taking the words right out of her mouth. Mrs. Graves and her grandmother had been good friends. She'd been eating her cookies since she was a little girl.

"Well, good. I'm glad you like them."

"Your car is all set."

The woman nodded and followed him into the garage.

"See you later, Mrs. Graves," Danica called over to her.

She waved and looked over her shoulder. "Take care, dear."

Danica watched as Jaden escorted her out to her car. As he stood there, she admired his confident strides and listened to his rumble as he laughed. Everything about him exuded a sexy air, and as a woman, no matter how hard she tried not to, she noticed. Danica felt a yearning but she was determined to keep her emotions in control around him and quickly shook it off and busied herself sorting invoices again. At the back of her mind, she was starting to think that maybe trying to draw Jaden's attention wasn't a smart move after all.

It was noon and the other two had already left for lunch when Jaden finally slid the creeper from beneath a Lincoln Town Car and reached for a rag to mop his forehead. He hadn't seen Danica for most of the morning and had a suspicion that she was purposely avoiding him. His gaze shifted to the reception area and he noticed that Shannon Jackson had come to pick up his black Hummer. The man had a reputation of being a womanizer. They had attended high school together, but Shannon wasn't particularly someone he would have considered a friend. Everyone knew the only person Shannon cared about was Shannon.

Jaden waited impatiently for Danica to signal his arrival. But instead of coming to get him, she stood at the counter engrossed in a conversation. His nostrils flared with a flash of anger and unfounded jealousy curled within him. He could tell by the way Danica was smiling that she was enjoying every minute of it. Shannon rubbed his chin and leaned in closer the way he did whenever he was ready to make a score, which meant his latest prey was Danica.

Why do you care?

He briskly dragged a hand across his locks. The question taunted him, but was one he was not prepared to answer. He had no claims on Danica, and she had the right to date whomever she wanted, but there was no way in hell he was going to stand back and let her get mixed up with someone as sneaky as Shannon Jackson.

Determined to interrupt, he headed across the garage, anxious to get Shannon his keys and send him on his way. Jaden stepped into the reception area in time to see Shannon passing Danica his business card, and to hear her promising to give him a call.

"Your Hummer's ready."

Danica glanced briefly over at Jaden before returning her attention to Shannon. "Oh, what a shame! I was enjoying our conversation," she said with a playful pout.

Shannon licked his lips. "Call me. I'll be more than happy to finish our conversation."

"I'll do that," she replied.

Jaden walked him out to the car, then waited until Shannon pulled off before he returned to the reception area where Danica was gathering her things.

"Well, I'm out of here," she said and didn't even bother to look his way. "I'll see you tomorrow."

Crossing his arms, he stood and observed her. He didn't know why it angered him that she didn't look at him the way she had at Shannon. "Do me a favor, and wear something a little less revealing tomorrow."

Danica's eyes snapped up to meet his, and Jaden caught the exact moment her temper began to flare.

"Revealing?"

"Yes, revealing. This is a place of business, not a pickup joint. If you're going to be fraternizing with the customers, then I'd rather you not come back tomorrow."

"I wasn't *fraternizing!* That's called good customer service."

"Good customer service doesn't include exchanging phone numbers."

"What I do with my personal life is none of your business," she said with a rude snort.

"You are my business," Jaden said slowly, studying her. "At least while you're working for me." He moved forward until there were mere inches separating them.

With Jaden looking at her in that intent brooding way, those thick eyebrows drawn together as if he was seeing through her, Danica decided it was time to make certain he understood she was no longer his business. But her eyes shifted, and she made the mistake of looking at his mouth and started to tremble. The last thing she wanted to do was to be standing there, thinking about those sensual lips pressed against hers. He was standing way too close, making her completely aware of him.

"Go ahead. Tell me what's running through your mind. Regret walking out on a fine brotha like myself?" He reached up and stroked her hair.

"Not on your life."

"Liar."

Danica wondered how she could even think about forgiving him, but right now all she could think about was kissing him. "I'm not lying," she said and looked up at him, refusing to cower even though his touch made her quiver at the knees.

"So you're saying you've never once thought about what we had?"

Sensation raced through her as his eyes intensified. "Never."

"You're lying." He combed his fingers through her hair, and she found herself tilting her face toward his hand. "I guarantee when the time is right, you'll tell me the truth."

Truth! That was something he knew nothing about. *Snap out of it.* It took every ounce of willpower to push his hand away. "I've already told you the truth! I'm engaged to someone else. As far as I'm concerned our relationship is in the past and, if we're going to work together, you need to worry about fixing my car and let me do my job." She took a deep breath, her voice shakier than she wanted.

Jaden chuckled, and she knew at that instant he was fully aware of the effect he still had over her. "Then I guess I'll see you in the morning."

"I guess you will!" she snapped, then spun on her heels but stopped halfway and pivoted to look at him. "Just remember we have a deal, Jaden Beaumont. Tomorrow, I'll start reviewing applications and as soon as my car is fixed you don't have to worry about seeing me or my *fraternizing* behavior again." With that said, Danica stormed out of the building.

After she was gone, Jaden shook his head and raked a hand across his hair. He couldn't help thinking that maybe he had overreacted. All morning he tried to keep her at a distance and found it to be more difficult than he had imagined. Her perfume filled the garage. Her beauty was almost impossible to ignore. His sanctuary at work had been disrupted by a woman whose skin had been warm to the touch, whose eyes were soft brown or honey depending on her mood. Jaden wanted more than anything to taste her mouth again. But the last thing he needed to do was to travel down that road. Danica had already proven that she was not to be trusted with his heart. But he had seen in her eyes that she still wasn't as immune to him as she pretended to be. If he had kissed her, would it have proven how she really felt? Dammit, the last thing he needed was to resurrect old feelings. But one thing he did know: if they were going to continue to work together, then it was time for them to put their differences behind them and somehow come to some kind of understanding.

Chapter 5

"Damn that man!" Danica screamed.

That would be the last time she ever set foot in his garage again. She stormed through her house, cursing under her breath. The man was simply impossible. The nerve of him treating her like a tramp. *Who does he think he is?*

Taking the stairs two at a time, she hurried up to her room anxious to change into something comfortable so she could get over to the boutique and relieve Nyree. Just thinking about the entire morning she had wasted on a man who didn't even appreciate her help caused her to kick and send her pumps flying across the room. Oh, she was mad. *Hot!*

The morning hadn't gone anything at all as she had planned. Jaden was supposed to have been falling all over himself trying to get her attention. He was supposed to beg her to give him another chance. Instead, he turned the tables and had her yearning for his touch. His kiss. Now she was so pissed off she was seconds away from bursting a blood vessel or two. How dare he imply that she was flirting with the customers? Okay, so maybe she had gone a bit overboard with the *customer service*. But nevertheless, who was he to assume she was fraternizing?

Maybe he's jealous.

As she moved over to an oak armoire, Danica took a second to mull over the idea, and half a smile tilted her lips. Maybe her plan had worked after all. That meant she would have to go back again tomorrow and give him an even heavier dose. A frown wrinkled her brow. Damn, she had no intention of returning, yet as much as that man pissed her off, the two of them had a deal and there was no way in hell she would ever allow him to label her a quitter. No way. She shrugged out of her jacket and let it fall freely to the floor. She unzipped her skirt and it also landed in the same pile. All she wanted to do now was change clothes and get over to the boutique so she could make up for lost time.

The house phone rang, interrupting any further foolish thoughts. She moved over to the side of her bed and grabbed it.

"Where have you been? I've been calling you all morning!"

Vertical lines appeared between her dark, expressive eyes. Goodness gracious, the last person she wanted to talk to right now was her overly dramatic older sister, Maureen. "I'm spending the next two weeks helping a…uh…" Danica paused for a moment "…friend out in the mornings."

"Helping out? How do you have time to help out when you're trying to open in less than a month?" she questioned.

"Crazier things have happened. One of them being the engine in Daddy's car going out."

"Oh no. You love that car!"

Danica sighed and reached inside her drawer for a pink T-shirt. "Which is why I'm helping out a mechanic in exchange for him fixing Daddy's car at a reduced price."

"Reduced? That sounds kind of fishy to me. Is he desperate?"

"Hardly," she replied while pulling the shirt over her head.

"Then he must be fine?" she asked.

Glancing at her reflection in the mirror, Danica let out a breath in an audible sigh. "Very."

"Ooh! Please do tell."

"What's there to tell? He's gorgeous and in desperate need of an assistant, and I'm desperate to get my car fixed. End of story."

Maureen snorted rudely into the receiver. "I don't believe that for a second, and neither do you. Danica, it's time for you to start dating again and get over that fool Jarred."

"His name is Jaden."

"Yeah, well, whatever his name is, it's time for you to give love a second chance and it sounds like this man has potential."

Danica groaned inwardly. She would be so glad when her sister found a man of her own and stopped trying to live vicariously through her life. "Maureen... Jaden's the one repairing my car."

Her statement was met by silence over the line.

That'll shut her up. It took everything she had not to laugh. "Maureen, you still there?"

"I'm here. Have you lost your mind?"

No, but I'm in jeopardy of losing my heart again if I'm not careful. "No. It's a business agreement. Nothing more."

"A business agreement? Have the two of you talked about what happened?"

"No, and we're not going to. It's better to just leave the past in the past. Some people aren't meant to be together, and we are those people."

"Maybe so, but even if he isn't the one, there is someone else out there for you."

"I doubt that."

"Everyone has a soul mate," Maureen added in a soothing voice.

She had thought the same thing. The chemistry between her and Jaden had led to a passion that burned hot every time they were together. Over the weeks their relationship had only grown stronger, and the torch never once blew out. Then their lust became hot and emotional as well. It was funny because before she met him, she had sworn not to change her life for any man. Her career as a model was all she had cared about. She refused to turn out like her mother, who had given up her dreams of being a lawyer to become the wife of a marine and spent twenty years following him around the world until he joined the fire department. Not Danica, no way. She wanted to never look back and wonder shoulda, coulda, woulda.

And then she had fallen in love with Jaden, and for the first time in her life, she understood what her mother meant when she said she never had any regrets. Love and her children were all she could ever have hoped for. As far as her mother had been concerned, nothing made her happier than to have had someone to grow old with. That happiness had lasted almost forty years before the Lord decided it was time to take her mother home. Danica had wanted the same thing with Jaden and was willing to join him in California and give up her dream of opening a boutique on the Delaware shore. She'd never forget the way she cried when Jaden cradled her in his arms and stared down tenderly into her eyes as he confessed how much he loved her. Then the next day her entire world came crumbling down when she found out it had all been a game. The moment she confessed to Jaden that she loved him, too, he had won his five-hundred-dollar prize. Never again would she allow herself to be that vulnerable to a man.

Maureen cleared her throat, bringing her mind back to the present.

"I don't think so, sis," Danica said as she made her way over to the closet and pulled out a pair of worn jeans.

Maureen sighed heavily in her ear. "Well, at least get yourself some."

"What?"

A throaty female laugh came through the wire. "I didn't stutter. Get some."

"Oh brother, not that again," she moaned as she pulled the jeans over one leg then the other.

"You told me once that was the best sex you ever had. Then, fine, get you some because you're getting crabby!"

"Okay, I'm hanging up," Danica warned between clenched teeth.

"Fine, but you know what I'm saying is true. Just be careful."

She couldn't help but laugh. "I will."

They talked a few more minutes about their older brother, Kenyon, who was serving over in Iraq, and then she hung up and moved into the bathroom. As she splashed water on her face, she couldn't help thinking about what Maureen had said. Sex wasn't a bad idea at all. It was the emotional attachment she would have trouble separating herself from.

Danica spent the afternoon ordering merchandise for her boutique. She planned to have swimsuits to fit women of all shapes and sizes because she believed that a woman should feel sexy no matter what her size.

All the shelves had been installed on the tangerine-colored walls. The first shipment of merchandise was due in by the end of next week. The boutique would have flip-flops and scarves for the waist, as well as accessories such as sunglasses and sunscreen.

By sundown Danica was tired, but pleased with the progress. If she kept up her pace she would be ready for her grand opening in less than four weeks.

"So this is your boutique?"

She swung around to find Jaden coming through the door. At the sight of him, her chest tightened. He was the last person she expected to see and she tried to hide her surprise, but it was useless. Confident, relaxed, his penetrating gaze burned Danica as if he could see beneath her clothes. She fought the urge to fold her arms across the chest to protect herself from the power of his gaze.

Her surprise quickly turned into a frown. "Jaden."

"Danica." She knew the smile he gave her was just to infuriate her. "Very impressive."

He closed the door behind him, locking it, then turned and headed over to where she was sitting in the middle of the floor, his gaze never once straying from hers. Her chest tightened with every step he took toward her. The room was too small for the two of them. She suddenly was aware that they were sharing the same air. At his garage they had an excuse to be together. Now was a different story altogether.

"Danica, the normal response to a compliment is thank you."

She took a deep breath while reminding herself not to let him get to her, which wasn't easy, considering he was getting to her in more ways than one. "Thank you." She rose, dusted off her jeans and made herself meet his eyes. He had cleaned up. The oily work clothes were gone and in their place were clean jeans and an orange T-shirt. She loved a man in orange. *And he knows it.*

"What are you doing here?" she asked impatiently. The sooner she got rid of him the better.

Jaden shrugged. He was so relaxed and in control as always. That was when he was his most dangerous. His eyes never shifted from her face. Nervously, she reached up and tried to mend her unruly ponytail. "I was strolling down the beach and saw your light on. Thought I'd stop by and see how things were going." Looking to his left, he spotted a pitcher of iced water and plastic cups on the table. "Mind if I help myself? I'm a little thirsty."

"No, go ahead," she murmured, watching as he moved over and reached for a glass. She was struck by how well he filled out a pair of jeans. *Uh, uh, uh!* She had always been a butt man, and Jaden definitely had a nice one.

Once the cool water sated his thirst, Jaden tossed the

cup in the trash and turned back to where she was sitting. "You need some help?" he offered.

She shook her head. The last thing she needed was him invading her space. "No. I'm almost done."

"You know it's after ten o'clock."

"Ten!" She glanced down at her watch. Where in the world had the time gone? "I guess I better go home fairly soon and get some rest if I'm going to make it into the garage on time."

"I'll hang around till you're done and walk you home," he offered.

She looked over at him and frowned. "I can manage."

"Don't get me wrong, Sheraton Beach is one of the safest towns in the country, but it will make me feel a lot better knowing I made sure you got home safely." He moved toward her and she knew it was pointless to argue. As he drew nearer, her body suddenly came alive and vibrated, and then heat traveled through and settled down between her thighs.

Fine. Hang around if you want to. She tried to concentrate on her ordering, but she could not keep her train of thought. Danica groaned inwardly. He was definitely too much of a distraction. Out the corner of her eye, she watched as Jaden took a seat in a nearby folding chair and glanced around the room before bringing his gaze back to her face.

"This is a really nice setup. What made you decide to open a boutique?"

"I decided I needed to do something when I visited the shops on the boardwalks and none of them offered any of the designs I endorsed."

He reached for one of the designs she had lying on top of a box on the table. "I saw you in this one." It was a two-piece lemon-colored swimsuit that offered built-in support.

She smiled at his memory. While in California he had attended a photo shoot she had done for *Cosmopolitan* magazine. "You've got a good memory."

"I haven't forgotten anything about us."

Their eyes locked for a long, intense moment before she lowered her eyes to the floor. Jaden's look unsettled her. Not interested in discussing the past, Danica decided it was time to call it a night. The sooner she put some distance between them the better. "Let me grab my purse. As soon as I turn out the lights I'll be ready to go."

He rose and tucked his hands in the pockets of his jeans while he waited. She was trembling as she moved to her office in back, retrieved her purse and slipped on her sweater. The nights were always cool along the ocean. It took her five minutes to turn out all the lights and set the alarm before locking the door behind her.

She turned to face him, and Jaden probed her eyes before saying, "Ready?"

She nodded.

He reached out a hand, almost daring her to take it. Like his body, hard and rough, his callused fingers were the ones that once cupped her breasts, had parted her wet flesh and held her tightly in his arms. She tried to push the memories aside.

It's just his hand, that's all.

Like some drug, his eyes sapped her will to resist and lured her into submission.

Hand in hand they walked along the sandy beach. She enjoyed the slight breeze ruffling her hair. There was no need for words. Instead they were both lost in their thoughts, savoring the warmth of the night.

In the distance boats bobbed, moored to a pier. Danica inhaled the salty air and allowed herself just a few minutes to enjoy the moment. She had always loved the smell of the ocean. It was so different from growing up in a big city like Richmond.

Before she realized it, they had left the beach and had turned onto her street.

"I've always liked this neighborhood," Jaden said, breaking the comfort of their silence.

She glanced over at him. He was looking straight ahead so she took a moment to stare at his strong profile under the glow of a streetlight. "I've always liked it, as well." They had entered the historical district of the community. Large Victorian-style homes with wide wraparound porches. She often imagined what it had been like for her mother growing up here.

Danica pointed to a large white house across from them. "Did I ever tell you my father lived there?"

Jaden looked over at her and shook his head.

She nodded, her lips curling upward at the memories. "Daddy grew up on one end of the street and Mama on the other. They knew each other all their lives. Mama used to tell stories of how they couldn't stand each other. Daddy was two years older than her, but very immature. He use to throw spitballs at her in school, and snowballs when he spotted her and her friends walking down the street together. Mama said he made her so mad that one day she waited behind a car for him to pass and tossed a brick at his head."

He chuckled. "No way!"

"Yep, she sure did," Danica continued with a giggle. "She only tried to scare him, but when he started crying and she saw all that blood, she raced home to get my grandmother. They rushed him to the emergency room, and Mama held his hand while they gave him eight stitches. They were inseparable ever since."

"How old were they then?"

She smiled up at him. "Twelve. Daddy said that even then he knew Mama was the only woman he wanted to spend the rest of his life with."

They were quiet the rest of the walk and when they reached the large house with the soft lemon siding, Jaden opened the gate and walked her up to the door. Danica put the key in the lock and opened it before turning to Jaden. A slow smile trembled over her lips. "Thanks for walking me home."

"Any time," he replied softly into the night. Jaden filled in the distance separating them, standing toe-to-toe. So close she could feel the warmth of his body. "Danica, I want to apologize for what I said earlier. It was totally out of line. If we're going to work together, then I want us to at least try and be friends."

She nodded. "I'd like that." His hand settled on her upper arm and she began to shiver. Capturing the look in his eyes, she heard one thing and saw something totally different. Warning bells went off in her head, and Danica tried to back away.

Jaden's breath feathered the tip of her nose. "What are you afraid of?" he asked in that deep, seductive voice of his. The moonlight caught the glint of his eyes beneath those long eyelashes.

"I'm not afraid of anything," she answered nervously. Oh, she was lying through her teeth. She was afraid all right. Afraid of what she might allow him to do. Her yearning for him was too strong and she didn't know if she'd be able to resist if she gave in to the temptation. "I just don't think this is a good idea."

He leaned in until their lips were almost touching. "Too bad. I think it's a wonderful idea."

Before she could protest, Jaden swooped in and kissed her. She tried pressing her lips firmly together, but Jaden slid his tongue along the sill until her mouth relaxed and she accepted him. As soon as she did, he moved inside, taking possession of exactly what he wanted. Oh, but the things this man could do to her! She couldn't think. She could barely breathe as he took her in a long deliberate kiss. Danica placed a hand on his chest, preparing to push away, but he must have known what she was about to do because he reached for her waist, encircling his arm around her and pulling her close. A little moan escaped her lips and that was all the invitation Jaden needed. He took complete advantage and it became useless to refuse. Her tongue met his and instead of pulling away, Danica found herself surrendering to the moment as she molded her body to his.

Jaden hadn't known what he was after when he stepped into her boutique. Now he knew. He wanted to sample her mouth, and once he had, he had the strong need to know if she tasted the same.

She didn't.

Danica tasted better.

How many times had he thought about kissing her? Holding her in his arms? More times than he really cared to remember. And now that he was holding her, touching her, smelling a scent that belonged uniquely to her, he was in a state of arousal like no other. Immense heat swamped him and his groin tightened. Jaden growled against her mouth. He had always been a weak man with little self-control where Danica was involved. Tonight was no exception.

Leaning forward, Danica pressed the swell of her breasts against his chest. And the feel of her hardened nipples was enough to bring him to his knees. His mind started playing tricks on him and he envisioned carrying her inside and finishing where they had left off eighteen months ago. Jaden buried his fingers in her hair. Danica gasped and her hold tightened.

"Danica," he whispered, then rained kisses along her neck and jaw.

Danica seemed to melt into his arms. She drew his mouth back to hers. Their kiss was full of delicious yearning.

Following a moan, Jaden slid his hand down, searching for, and finding, the curve of her breast. He then followed the indention of her waist and the flare of her hips. She was perfect just the way he remembered.

He backed her against the door and kissed her the way he used to. Danica arched her back, giving him better access. He could feel the rapid beat of her heart and he knew he needed to stop before it got out of hand. Her legs parted to cradle him and all thoughts of stopping vanished. Instead, with his lips never leaving hers, he moved them into the darkest corner of the porch. His fingers slipped beneath her shirt, giving him better access to her beautiful full breasts.

He had spent many restless nights dreaming of them, remembering their softness, remembering the chocolate nipples. While he continued to caress her breasts, he slipped his other hand inside her loose-fitting jeans. His fingers trekked slowly, teasing until he finally found her.

Danica broke off the kiss. "Jaden, no."

"Yes," he practically growled, then silenced any further protest with kisses.

Once again she became his willing partner. He could feel her heat, even through all the layers of their clothes. He hadn't felt this urgent desire before in his life. It was maddening but he needed to touch her. To taste her.

He felt the waistband of her soft panties and slipped his hand inside and released a frustrated groan when he found her moist. Instinctively, Danica rocked into him. Her arms around his neck tightened. For one incredible moment, she was compliant in his arms; then with enough force, she finally pushed him away.

"Stop!" Her voice shook with the same unfulfilled passion that drove him.

It was then that he realized how far he had gone. If she hadn't stopped him he would have taken her right there outside on the porch. He had her back against the door with his knee between her legs. One hand down her pants. The other covering her breast.

Jaden released her and placed his hands on the door on either side of her head. He then leaned in once more and seared her with a heated kiss. "Get inside before I carry you into the house and finish what you started."

Her eyes grew round with rage. "I've started? You're the one—"

He cut her off. "Danica, go inside. Now!"

She must have seen how serious he was, because she nodded and quickly slipped through the door and shut it behind her.

Inside the house, Danica locked the door and sank against it, willing herself not to break down.

Over Jaden?
No way!

Breathe in. Breathe out. All she needed was a moment to get herself together. Taking several more deep breaths, she tried to ignore her heart pounding, her body throbbing with need.

When Jaden ordered her to get inside the house, she saw the desire and anger. Before she scrambled inside, she had witnessed the muscles working at his jaw, which was why she had obeyed and hurried into the house. Not because she was afraid of Jaden, but because she didn't trust herself around him.

Dear God, she missed being touched, missed the feel of a man's arms, *his* arms. How long had it been? Too damn long. Yet despite all those months apart, Danica never would have dreamed she would have given in to Jaden so easily.

Damn him! She pushed away from the door and headed up to her bedroom.

He wasn't playing fair and knew it. He was trying to go back to the way things were. Well, she wasn't having it. For months she had kept those memories pushed to the side, refusing to wallow in self-pity and think about a relationship that had been nothing more than a game. Their past had no part in her new life. Her present was just as she wanted it, and with her boutique opening soon the future looked even brighter. And Jaden was not now, nor would he ever be, a part of any of that.

She hurried up to her room, then took a seat on the bed and slipped her sandals off. Reaching for her slippers under the bed, she released a heavy sigh of despair. Just being around Jaden, she felt him slowly crumbling that tall concrete wall she had put up around her emotions. But damn, she was not going to make it easy for him.

Teasing him with what he was missing had not been a smart move. She knew that now. Jaden was a man, and a man wants what a man wants. Showing him what he was missing only caused him to want to take up where they had left off, which wasn't remotely possible. Yet, after that kiss, she now knew she wasn't immune to him. The safest thing for her was to keep her distance until her car was done and a receptionist had been hired.

What the hell was wrong with him? Jaden thought with an angry scowl as he moved down the long path to his small oceanfront house. He'd had no business kissing Danica Dansforth. He'd gotten his heart tangled up with her before and had it ripped from his chest. Hadn't he learned his lesson?

I guess not.

Being around her, all he could do was think about touching and kissing her and all afternoon he had been overwhelmed with a strong need to see if she still tasted as good as he had remembered. *Dammit!* Being around her stirred up all kinds of emotions inside him and it irritated the hell out of him how much he still wanted her.

Goodness, one suggestive word out of her mouth was all it took to make him hard. After all these months, one look, one touch and he wanted to carry her to bed so he could kiss her, caress her breasts and drive into her until she screamed his name. He'd never forgive her for using him, yet that did nothing to simmer the sexual ache he had inside.

Once he opened the front door, Jaden headed straight for the kitchen and retrieved a bottle of beer, then moved out onto a small wooden deck where he had a magnificent view of the ocean. An hour and three beers later, he tipped his chair back and propped his feet on the railing while cursing under his breath. Dammit, he tried to act as though he didn't care. Why should he? Danica turned out not to be the type of woman he had thought her to be. *So why am I sitting here thinking about her?* For crying out loud, she was engaged to someone else, which meant she was off-limits. But that didn't mean he didn't want to make love to her, he thought as he popped the tab on another can. Just being around her, smelling her hair, catching a wisp of her natural scent that still lingered on his clothes, charged him with restless energy. But that didn't mean anything other than that he was a man.

Jaden scrubbed a rough, callused hand across his face and inhaled the salty air. Even now he could feel the sweet pressure of her firm breasts, her inviting mouth. She'd been a wonderful temptation. But he had learned the hard way, heat and passion was only a temporary relief. He'd be a fool to jump back into bed with her. Last time she had taken what she had wanted, then kissed him goodbye and never looked back.

He wouldn't be played for a fool again no matter how badly he wanted her.

Chapter 6

"Danica is doing a good job of running that front desk," Kyle commented as he handed Jaden a wrench.

Even though he didn't bother to reply, his heart sped up a beat at the mention of her name.

It had been two days since he walked her home, sealing the night with a kiss. Ever since he'd been doing everything he could to avoid her presence, which wasn't the easiest thing to do with the two of them working together. However, he had tried to make a habit of staying in the garage until after she left each afternoon for the boutique.

He knew how well she was managing the front office from Kyle, who looked forward to drinking a cup of her perfectly brewed coffee each morning. But even though he kept his distance, there were plenty of things that made her presence known. One being the soft floral scent of her perfume that filled the reception area long after she was gone. Another was the notes she left for him in her neat scripted handwriting at the end of each shift, detailing the day's activities.

The last two days hadn't been completely hard because she, too, appeared to be avoiding him. Every afternoon she quietly slipped out of the shop without ceremony. Any questions she directed to either Kyle or Tim, who had finally gotten used to her being around. The first time she ignored Jaden, it had angered him. After that he decided that it was probably for the best. Yet no matter how much he tried to ignore her, he found himself looking through the glass into the reception area each time he got eager for at least a glimpse of the auburn beauty. He knew he had to keep himself busy or else he would be checking on her every ten minutes and he didn't want to appear intrigued in front of Kyle and Tim, because those two were way too observant. The only time he had to himself was after they were gone, but by then Danica had left, as well.

The worst part was at night, when he'd lie awake in his bed with images of her dancing beneath his eyelids as he relived every intimate detail of the kiss they had shared. The taste of her lips. The feel of her lush body in his arms. The way she moaned when he grazed her nipple with his thumb. The worst part about it was that he wanted Danica back in his bed.

Desperate to rid his mind of her, he had gone out last night hoping to run into one of his exes or stumble across a new squeeze. But every available woman in that club was a poor substitute for the real thing, and even after getting several offers to "rock his world" he went home alone. For some crazy reason his body refused to settle for less. The only woman he wanted to sleep with had just left for the boutique fifteen minutes ago.

His stomach growled loudly, interrupting his raging thoughts.

"Hungry, boss?"

Jaden moved away from the car and reached for a rag. It took him several seconds to remember when was the last time he had eaten. He realized he hadn't had anything since lunch the day before.

"Yeah," he began as he wiped his hands. "I'll run out in a few minutes."

"Go. Go ahead now. I think me and Tim can handle it."

He gave him a stern look and a lifted brow. "Are you trying to get rid of me?"

"Yep," Kyle replied without hesitation. "You've been grouchy all morning. Maybe a little food and some fresh air will put you in a better mood."

Jaden didn't bother to argue. Instead he moved toward the reception area and made a beeline for the bathroom to wash his hands. Kyle was right. He had been in a sour mood the last couple of days and he knew the reason why.

Danica.

He lathered his hands twice, then reached for a paper towel and dried them off and tossed the wet paper into the trash. As he moved through the door he ran smack into someone and it took a few seconds for the haze to clear before he realized it was Danica.

"Sorry about that," he said in an apologetic voice, then glanced down at his wristwatch. "I thought you left already?"

She seemed just as surprised to see him. "I left my cell phone and came back to get it."

"Oh," he replied, then allowed his eyes to travel over her outfit that he had admired from afar all morning. Blue-jean skirt and a blue blouse that hugged all her curves. As usual she was wearing very little makeup. Danica was fresh, feminine and downright sexy as hell. Her stomach growled and he bit back a chuckle. "It sounds like we're both hungry."

She gave an easy smile. "I'll grab something on the way to the boutique."

He looked down at her and felt that same sizzle he always felt around her. "Have lunch with me?"

She hesitated before finally shaking her head. "Nyree's waiting for me."

Drawn as if by a magnet, his gaze locked with hers. This was the woman he had spent the last several nights dreaming about. This was the woman whose taste still lingered on his tongue. This was the woman he desperately wanted to make love to. Staring down at her, he realized that as foolish at it might seem, he wanted to spend the next hour with her. "Call and tell her you'll be late."

Her spine stiffened noticeably. She never did like for someone to tell her what to do. "I don't think so."

"I insist. I'll buy you lunch for my appreciation for everything you've been doing around here."

"I'm only holding up my end of the deal."

She was so stubborn sometimes that he wanted to toss her over his knees and spank her. The mere thought gave him a serious hard on.

"Danica, all I'm asking for is lunch and then I'll give you a lift down to the pier."

Her eyes grew thoughtful and she nibbled nervously on her lip before she finally agreed. Jaden went and retrieved his keys before she had a chance to change her mind.

Jaden called Clarence's Chicken and Fish House and ordered two lunch specials, then took Danica by the arm and escorted her out to his Denali. What was the point of saying no? She knew Jaden well enough to know that refusing his invitation was one fight she was destined to lose. When Jaden wanted something, he usually got it. Her thoughts started to dwell on their failed relationship and she couldn't help but sum up that everything—in her case, everyone—was a challenge to him. Unfortunately that was all their relationship had ever amounted to.

Danica gazed out the window, trying her hardest not to focus on the man sitting beside her. But out of the corner of her eye, she couldn't help but admire his locks that were pulled back in a ponytail, drawing attention to his handsome face.

The last two days had been pure torture. She had been doing everything in her power to avoid him. Arriving at the garage after he was already under the hood and leaving right at lunchtime. Her advantage was that they had been so busy. Jaden was so compassionate in his work that he rarely stopped for air. Yet every night was spent lying awake yearning for his touch. Today she had suspected he, too, was avoiding her and was irritable. It was too obvious not to notice. She'd have to be deaf not to hear Jaden snapping at Kyle and Tim for the littlest thing. She also knew the reason had everything to do with the kiss they had shared. Well, there was no reason for him to be angry. He was the one who kissed her, not the other way around. What Jaden Beaumont needed to do was learn to keep his lips to himself.

"You don't realize how much something meant to you until it is gone."

"What?" Abruptly, his words captured her attention.

Jaden took his eyes away from the road long enough to grant her an irresistible smile. "Being home. I didn't realize how much I missed this place until I got back here."

She dropped her eyes to her lap. For a brief, foolish moment, Danica thought he was talking about her. "I know what you mean. How does it feel being back?"

An easy smile curled his lips. "Good. Damn good. I don't think I'll ever leave again."

She nodded in agreement. "This place does have that kind of affect on you. I remember when I was a kid I couldn't wait to come here every summer. I always felt like I was at peace here. I still do."

His smile widened. "I know. I've always felt like that here."

She was glad they'd found a safe topic to discuss. "Then why did you leave?"

Jaden released a heavy breath and headed toward downtown before answering. "I wanted to find my own way. My parents were smothering. The Beaumont Hotel is their life and my father made it clear since I was old enough to read, he wanted all of his children to follow in his footsteps. The hotel industry was never something that interested me, but Roger Beaumont never wanted to hear that and never would have given me his blessing for any of the other choices I made. I knew that I had to get away from here at least long enough to find my own way."

She slanted a glance at his rugged profile. "And that's when you joined the army?"

He nodded. "Yep. I broke the news of my enlistment to my parents the day after graduation. My father flipped and my mother faked a heart attack."

Giggling, Danica turned slightly on the seat. As foolish as she knew it was, she needed to see his lips as he spoke.

"I did three years before I realized a career in the military was not for me. My father was certain that I was finally ready to come home and take my place at the hotel, but that was not happening," he said with a hearty chuckle. "Wearing a suit and tie had never been my thing."

Danica nodded although she remembered the way he looked in a tuxedo at his brother's wedding. Her mouth had watered. The suit had clearly been made just for him. "How'd you end up in California?"

"I had been stationed in California and loved it, so I decided to stick around and take some of the trust fund my grandfather left me and opened my own garage."

While visiting him in California, Danica had had the opportunity to see the impressive full-service garage. "Did you keep it?"

He shook his head. "No. I let it go. Trying to manage a business on the West Coast would have been too hard. I'd had someone wanting to buy it for a while and sold it before I had a chance to think about what I was doing."

"Any regrets?"

"None. What about you? You regret giving up modeling?"

She shook her head. "No way. I haven't felt this free in a long time."

He nodded in agreement. "I know exactly how you feel."

Obeying the twenty-mile-an-hour speed limit, Jaden pulled onto Main Street. Danica's eyes traveled along the wide cobblestone street that was lined with single-story buildings and mom-and-pop stores. Spring was off-season for the merchants of Sheraton Beach, who were anxiously awaiting the Memorial Day weekend, which would mark the start of their peak season. The town catered to tourists and by summer, the streets would be crowded and hotels sold out clear through Labor Day.

Jaden pulled up in front of Clarence's Chicken and Fish House and left the motor running while he ran inside. As soon as she was alone, she released a heavy breath. Damn, that man was fine. She would give anything to have him kissing her again, only this time she wanted the gesture to really mean something and not just be another one of his games.

Don't even go there.

All she wanted to do was help him identify a candidate, have her car fixed and get on with her life. Being around him conjured up too many emotions and memories that were best left alone.

She spotted Jaden coming out of the shop. He put the foam containers on the backseat and climbed in. Within seconds, the mouthwatering smell filtered through his SUV, making her stomach growl.

"I know exactly how you feel," Jaden said with a chuckle before he pulled away from the curb. Less than five minutes later, he turned into a parking spot a few feet away from her boutique and killed the engine.

"Thanks for the ride."

"Don't go. Please, keep me company while I eat my food."

Danica shifted on the seat. Common sense told her to decline his offer, grab her food and run. But the thought of spending a few more minutes with Jaden was too tempting to resist. She glanced over at the boutique before looking back over at him and nodded.

Jaden reached in back and retrieved the two containers and handed her one. Danica rested it on her lap and opened it up to fried catfish nuggets, home-style potatoes and corn bread. Hungrily, she popped a piece of fish into her mouth. "Mmm, I love his food."

"So do thousands of others. Old man Clarence has been around for a long time."

"And I can see why."

The seagulls sang overhead while the ocean roared in front them. Silence enveloped the vehicle. They were each too busy eating for conversation.

"What happened to us?"

His question caught her completely off guard, and Danica choked on a piece of fish.

"You okay?" Reaching over, he tapped her lightly on the back. She knew he was just trying to help, but his electrifying touch only made matters worse.

"I'm fine," she said and pushed his hand away. "I'm okay." Reaching down, she picked up her soda and took a thirsty swallow.

"Good. Then let's talk."

"Let's not," she managed between sips. "Some things are better left in the past."

"I disagree. I want to know why you decided all of a sudden to end our relationship, and most importantly why didn't you tell me you were engaged?"

She stared out at the ocean while she spoke. "I guess I wanted to make sure I wasn't making a mistake." Goodness, she hated lying.

"So are you saying that what we had wasn't real?"

"I didn't say that."

"Then what are you saying? Look at me, Danica."

Jaden reached up and cupped her chin and pinned her with his penetrating gaze, held her so she couldn't look away. She swallowed, stared into his hot, sable-brown eyes and fought not to tremble. She knew that determined look. She had seen it many times before, usually when he wanted something badly.

"You can't tell me that what we had wasn't real. I felt it and I know that you felt it, too. And as much as you might want to deny it, it's still alive and kicking between us. Come here." Before she realized what he was doing, he put their food on the backseat and pulled her across the seat and onto his lap, where he cradled her in his arms. He caught her hand, turned it over and kissed her palm, then flattened it to his chest, where she felt his heart pounding heavily. "Feel that? That's what you do to me."

Very slowly, Jaden lowered his mouth and captured her lips. Not a soft, gentle kiss but a hot, deep, demanding kiss that filled her with heat and need. Goodness, his warm, wet lips coaxed and demanded, giving and taking all at once. His tongue slid over her lips, sending warm shivers across her skin. She opened for him, inviting him inside. Her arms slid around his neck, pulling him closer.

"Tell me this isn't real." Jaden pressed his lips against the space below her ear, kissed the side of her neck, then captured her lips again. He loosened the buttons on her blouse and Danica moaned as he cupped her breast, his thumb stroking over her nipple. It swelled in his hand and caused her to arch against his palm.

"I never forgot about you. Never forgot about these," he said softly. Jaden caressed her other breast gently until her body throbbed with pleasure.

Danica knew she should stop him, but her own need pulsed to life with every stroke of his tongue, each feel of his hand against her breasts. She was faintly dizzy, breathing fast as he lowered his head and captured a hardened bud inside his mouth.

"Oh." A moan escaped her lips. She ran her fingers through his locks. She didn't know if she should push his head away or hold on. After months of yearning, she so desperately wanted, *needed,* what he was doing to her. His tongue circled her nipple as he suckled and tasted, sending little curls of heat sliding into her stomach and bursts to every limb in her body.

While he continued to suckle hungrily at her breasts, his hand slipped down past her belly, underneath her short denim skirt, to the juncture between her thighs, where he stroked along her satin crotch. Trembling, Danica tightened her hold on him.

From a distance she could hear laughter and children playing. And reality hit her. What in the world was she doing allowing him to practically make love to her in the front seat of his SUV? For all she knew this was another one of his bets. She pressed her hand against his chest, turned her head and struggled to be freed.

He gave her a puzzled look.

Shaking her head, she returned to the passenger's side and straightened up her blouse. "This is wrong. I'm engaged." She was breathing heavily.

Jaden gave a harsh look. "Engaged or not, we still have unfinished business and the sooner we deal with that the better."

Not bothering to respond, Danica grabbed her purse and food. Quickly, she climbed out and went inside, not once looking back.

Jaden reached for the remote control and turned on the basketball game. He had already missed the first half of the game, but it didn't matter. His mind was too far away to really care. What in the world was he thinking kissing Danica and demanding that she admit that what they once had was real? The operative word was *once*. Which meant it was best to leave well enough alone. Instead, he had tried to seduce her.

He released a string of choice words under his breath. He was asking for trouble.

He closed his eyes against the vision of Danica in the blue blouse and short denim skirt. She couldn't have looked more sexy if she'd been naked. Okay, maybe not naked, although he was certain she had no idea how good she looked. The soft material hugged her body rather than caressed it. The blue was rich and vibrant against her smooth skin.

What had gotten into him?

He wasn't sure. All he knew was after taking one look at her this afternoon as she swung her lush hips around the room that he had to have her. No ifs, ands or buts about it. Now he was supposed to work with her. Live in the same town and expect nothing to happen. *Right!* She made him feel things he did not want to feel, and that was a problem.

He rose from the couch, and with his hands embedded

in his pockets, he moved over to the window and stared out at the ocean view. The fog and the sounds of the waves marked a lonely night. It was evenings like this that he thought about what it would feel like to have someone sharing his life on a regular basis. Then as quickly as the fog lifted, so did the thought. But with Danica, it was becoming close to impossible to extract her from his mind.

Jaden rubbed a hand across his face. He was a confirmed bachelor. Women were good for sex and limited companionship, so why did being around Danica make him think about so many other things, as well? Why was he tempted to find a way to finally work her out of his system?

"Get a grip," he mumbled under his breath.

The phone rang. Glad for the distraction, he reached over on the coffee table for the cordless phone and brought it to his ear.

"Hello, dear."

Jaden silently groaned at the sound of his mother's high-pitched cultured voice. "Hello, Mother."

"I just had a disturbing conversation with Harriet."

And by the tone of her voice, he knew good and well he was the main topic of that conversation. "Oh, really, what about?" he asked, faking ignorance.

"Don't play with me, Jaden Joshua Beaumont, because I'm not in the mood today. How could you break Tiffany's heart like that?"

Shaking his head, he moved over to the couch and returned to his seat. "I didn't break her heart, Mother. She ended our relationship, not me."

"Because you refused to commit! Did you really think she would continue to just be a trophy on your arm? She's ready to settle down and have a family."

"Well, I'm not, which is why I agreed she is better off finding someone else." He should have known when Tiffany banged at his door a week ago giving him an ultimatum, which he ignored, she would go running to her grandmother, sobbing and pointing the blame. In fact, he was surprised it had taken this long for his mother to contact him.

"Jaden, sweetie. When are you going to settle down and start a family? I'm not getting any younger, you know," she finished with a dramatic sigh.

He found that bit of information ironic. Any other time and his mother swore she didn't look a day over fifty. "Mother, I'm barely twenty-seven and much too young to be thinking about marriage and babies. I'm sure Jabarie and Jace will be happy to give you all the grandchildren you'll ever need."

"Why are you being so unreasonable?" she retorted in a wounded voice. "You are my youngest son and it's time for you to settle down."

He rolled his eyes to the ceiling before he said between clenched teeth, "I'm sure in time, Mother, I will find the right woman. "

She sighed. "I never have been able to understand you."

He wanted to tell his mother that she would if she came down off her cloud and tried, but thought it best to keep that comment to himself.

"Are you coming to dinner on Thursday?" he heard her ask.

Like I have a choice. It had been a rule in their house since he was a little kid that no matter how busy they all were, the family always ate together on Thursday nights. Even after Jace and Jabarie had married, the tradition had continued. "Sure, what's Sylvia making?"

"Your favorite."

His mouth was already watering at the thought of having slow-cooked pot roast and mashed potatoes with homemade gravy. Sylvia had been cooking for their family long before he had said his first word. "I can't wait."

"Good, and we're having company for dinner."

He smelled a rat. "Who's coming?"

"Katherine's niece Stephanie is in town. I was hoping she could come so that we can all catch up," she gushed. "Did you know she speaks seven different languages fluently?"

How impressive. "Mother, please don't try and fix me up."

"I'm not. She just mentioned your name, and I thought it would be nice for the two of you to get reacquainted."

Great. Stephanie was a whiner and the last person he wanted to spend the evening with. "Mother, I'd rather not."

"Well then, Jaden, that leaves you two choices, either spend the evening sitting beside Stephanie or find a date of your own." Before he could respond, his mother hung up.

Great, just great. Now he had to produce a date or spend a long evening with Stephanie talking about all the countries she had lived in. Reaching for the beer can, he finished it in one swallow, then rose from the couch and grabbed is keys. He needed another six-pack.

After a long evening, she was glad to be home. Danica hurried up to her room and started stripping her clothes, then moved into the bathroom for a shower.

Twenty minutes later, she reemerged feeling relaxed and refreshed.

She loved her grandmother's two-story Victorian-style house, especially the master suite. Rich carpet the color of cognac lay on the floor of the master suite. Floor-to-ceiling windows were covered with drapes the color of sweet cream. Furniture was ornately carved out of light wood. She moved over to the large canopy bed in the middle of the room and slipped beneath bedding of soft down.

She closed her eyes and visualized Jaden's face. His mesmerizing eyes. Those thick, luscious lips. He was handsome, rugged and downright appealing. Memories returned with more details. The kissing. The lovemaking. She knew the weight of his body and knew the taste of his skin. The smartest thing for her to do was to stay far away from Jaden. He was making her feel things again that she didn't want to feel for him or any other man right now.

What if I made a mistake?

Sighing deeply, Danica turned onto her side. The way he had behaved this afternoon made her almost wonder if maybe she had been wrong. Could she have overheard him incorrectly? She pushed that thought aside. She knew what she had heard. He had betted on winning over a redhead and that woman was her.

Frustrated, she squeezed her eyelids shut and scolded herself for even taking the moment to second-guess her actions. Instead, she blamed Jaden for making her feel crazy these last few days. What was going on was clearly sexual.

Jaden had admitted he wanted to sleep with her. As crazy as it might sound, she was glad to know Jaden was

fighting his attraction for her as much as she was
fighting hers to him. She didn't want to admit it but she
would do anything for them to go back to the way things
once were. To find out that what he said he felt, he
really did feel. She was foolish to have even tried to
deny she was attracted to him. However, she would be
downright stupid if she gave in and considered doing
something about it. She reminded herself of what she
had gone through. The man she had loved hadn't really
loved her at all.

And that hurt.

As long as she reminded herself of the months it took
to repair her heart, she wouldn't have to worry about
finding herself once again in Jaden's bed.

Chapter 7

Two days later, Danica sat behind the counter, frowning.

She had spent the last hour reviewing applications. *What the hell?* These women weren't applying for a receptionist position. They were interested in being Mrs. Jaden Beaumont, Apparently as soon as word got out that he was looking for help, every available woman in town wanted to get close to the new owner.

Danica shook her head, trying to shake off the state she felt. She hated the feeling of jealousy that surrounded her. In all honesty her heart had never quite healed after her heartbreak. She thought she had dealt with it, and was over Jaden, but now, being around him, discovering that almost every woman in town wanted him, she had to face the fact that she hadn't. No, she truly believed she was no longer in love with him, but intense feelings for him were there, which meant the sooner she could get this project done and get away from him, the better.

A customer stepped through the door and she looked up ready with a greeting. There stood a beautiful Hispanic woman with long coal-black hair that brushed her middle back.

"Hi, may I help you?"

The woman gave her a smile that didn't quite reach her face. "I'm Martina Rios. I am here to interview for the receptionist position," she replied with a thick Hispanic accent.

Danica looked at the woman from head to toe. *You got to be kidding!* She was dressed more as if she were on her way to audition at one of the strip clubs that had recently populated the outskirts of town. The tight red dress barely contained her double Ds and the sandals she was wearing added at least five inches to her petite frame.

"Do you have an appointment?" Danica inquired, because she definitely didn't remember calling anyone that sounded like her over the phone.

"Yes," Martina said. "I spoke to Jaden this morning, or maybe it was last night," she added with a smirk.

That last comment struck a nerve and it took everything Danica had to keep a straight face. "Please have a seat. I'll let him know you are here." She turned on her heels and moved into the garage.

As soon as he heard her coming, Kyle stopped working and turned to greet her. Something on her face must have told him now was not the time, because her eyes grew large and round as he watched her storm over to where Jaden was changing a tire. She stopped and tapped her foot impatiently waiting for him to notice her.

"Hey," Jaden replied with a large smile.

For a moment she almost thought that their time together meant something, that they might possibly have another opportunity to get it right. *That's what you get for thinking.*

"Your ten o'clock appointment is here."

Jaden gave her a puzzled look. "Ten o'clock? I didn't know I was interviewing candidates today."

"Neither did I, but apparently you spoke to *Ms. Rios* on the phone this morning, or was it last night?" she said, harsher than she had intended. The last thing she wanted was for Jaden to know she was jealous.

Realization lit up his face. "Damn! I forgot about her."

"I just bet you did." She then turned on her heels and headed back into the front office.

A smirk curled Jaden's lips as he watched her leave. Danica was jealous. Good. That meant she still cared about him. What Danica didn't know was that the woman sitting in the lobby didn't hold a candle to her.

Kyle chuckled. "I think if she'd had a gun she would have shot you."

Tim slid from beneath an Impala, rose and brushed his pants off. "Did she say Martina Rios was in the lobby?"

"Yeah."

"Isn't she an ex of yours?" Tim asked Jaden inquisitively.

Kyle answered before he could. "Oh, yeah. Ms. Fatal Attraction is in the building."

The two chuckled. Ignoring them, Jaden moved toward the reception area. The sooner he got this over with the better.

He had dated Rios his senior year of high school. Everybody thought he had hit the jackpot when he landed the hottest girl in school. What they didn't know was that Martina was a possessive and crazy nut, who didn't know the meaning of no.

He stepped into the air-conditioned room and his eyes traveled over to Danica, who was standing behind the desk pretending she hadn't heard him enter.

"Jaden, *mi amor.*"

He turned in the direction of her soothing voice and found the beautiful woman coming toward him with a radiant smile. "Martina, please come back to my office."

As he moved toward the door, Jaden glanced over in Danica's direction and saw her roll her eyes before picking up the phone.

Jaden saw Kyle and Tim watching with interest as he and Martina moved across the garage toward his office. They were never going to let him live it down. He released a heavy sigh, then stepped in after Martina and closed the door behind them. He turned to face her. She leaned back against his desk suggestively.

"Martina, what do you want?"

"Like I told you last night, I'm interested in working here with you."

He dragged a hand through his locks, lifting them off his neck, wishing he had tied his hair up as he normally did. Last night he had received a private call shortly after midnight. It had been Martina asking him to come over and share her bed. As tempting as the offer was, he declined because it wouldn't have been a simple romp in the sack. Instead, he would have opened a whole new can of worms. And it just wasn't worth the drama.

"Martina, as I told you on the phone, the two of us working together is not a good idea."

"Why's that? I can type and answer phones. Hell, I spend the majority of my day on the phone."

Probably blowing up some poor unsuspecting brother's phone.

"We have a past and working with a woman I used to be…intimate with would not be a wise business move."

She paused as if thinking over what he said before she reached for his shirt and yanked him over so his body was pressed against her. "Fine, then I want the other job."

Jaden raised an eyebrow to the ceiling. "What other job?"

"I want to be your wife," she purred.

Danica angrily paced the floor of the lobby. "How dare he invite her here?"

An hour had passed since Jaden and Martina came out of his office and he escorted her out to her shiny new BMW, yet Danica was still fuming. Standing near the window, she had watched their interaction and it was almost apparent the two were either now sleeping together or had once been.

All that talk about what he was feeling and how much he missed her was all lies, because if he felt anything for her, there was no way he would have invited that…that woman in here.

Frowning, she moved over to the water fountain. She took a long drink, swallowed and released a long breath. Saying she was angry was an understatement. How dare he invite that woman here? Okay, so maybe she didn't have a right to be angry. After all, she had no claims on Jaden. It was the principle of the thing. Two days ago, he was trying to get her into bed and now he was trying to hire one of his "women" to work alongside him. All she wanted was her life back and as soon as she found him a receptionist she could leave.

The rest of the morning was relatively quiet. She scheduled two *legitimate* interviews, then worked on ordering parts for a 1998 Chevy Lumina.

Danica waited until after Kyle and Tim had left for lunch before she reached for her purse and headed into the garage to tell Jaden she was leaving. As soon as he saw her coming, he put his wrench on the hood of the car, reached for a rag and wiped his hands.

"How was the interview?" She forced the words through thick breath.

"She's not qualified," he replied with a wave of the hand.

She rolled her eyes. "I could have told you that and saved you the time."

He chuckled. "Why do you say that?"

Danica dropped a hand to her waist. "Because *Martina* isn't a receptionist, nor are any of the other candidates whose applications I have. They're nothing but a bunch of candidates wanting to be your baby's mama."

He gave her a strange look that said he didn't see what the problem was. "What's wrong with that?"

She jumped on that statement. "Everything! These are nothing but a bunch of hoochies looking for a husband or a quick fling."

"Sounds familiar, doesn't it?" He glared at her. "Isn't that what you wanted, a quick fling?"

"How dare you compare me to that tramp!" She took a swing but he blocked her fist.

Danica yanked free. Jaden chuckled and gave her an innocent look. "Hey, you started it, not me."

"You know what? Let's not even go there," she said then turned on her heels, but she wasn't quick enough.

He grabbed her arm. "No, let's."

She stared up at him and tried to focus on his chin, not his eyes.

"I want to know why," he said.

She took a deep impatient breath. "Why what?"

"Why didn't you tell me you were engaged?"

She groaned. Oh, no, they were not about to have this conversation again. "I thought you wanted me to find you a receptionist." She tried to jerk free, but Jaden held firmly to her forearm.

"That's not what I asked you." There was now a noticeable hard edge to his voice. "I want to know why in all the weeks we spent together, all the nights I was buried deep inside you, you never once mentioned you were engaged."

"I don't want to talk about it," she stuttered nervously.

"I do, and you owe me."

She jerked free. "*Owe you?* I don't owe you anything."

"The hell you don't."

Danica raked a frustrated hand across her curls. "After all this time why do you want to bring up the past? That was so long ago."

Jaden moved toward her and stopped with their feet touching. "It wasn't that long ago and you still haven't answered my question. I want to know why you didn't think it was important to tell me you were already promised to spend the rest of your life with another man."

She tossed her head back. "Would it have made a difference?"

He suddenly shoved both hands in his pockets. "Maybe, maybe not, but you took that option away from me."

"Then it's not important," she said with a slow shake of the head.

"Maybe to you it isn't."

She gaped. Did he mean it was important to him? She studied his face trying to find some sign of what he was feeling, but she saw nothing but the anger ticking at his jaw. Well, she was angry, too. How dare he act as if all this was her fault? Hell, if she hadn't overheard his conversation, there was no telling when she would have discovered that their relationship had been nothing more than a bet. "It's *your* fault we're not together, not mine. So don't even try and put this all on me."

His brow tilted. "*My* fault? How is this *my* fault?"

"It just is," she mumbled.

Jaden choked out a short laugh. "You're the one who left."

"I didn't leave," she retorted. "I told you I was going."

He gave her a disgusted look. "Oh, yeah, I almost forgot. You waited until I was carrying breakfast to bed to tell me you were leaving and, oh, by the way, I'm engaged," he barked mockingly. "Why?" he demanded as he pulled his hands from his pockets and crossed his arms over his chest. "Why the games?"

"Games? I wasn't playing games." If anyone had been playing games, it was Jaden. Remembering the humiliation, she got angry all over again.

Jaden grabbed her arm as she started to turn away

again. "Then what would you have called it? Why didn't you just tell me the truth?"

"Because…" The last thing she was going to do was talk about the past. It was bad enough he had stirred up unwanted feelings and emotions. The sooner she got away from him the better. "Listen, the last thing I'm going to do is stand here and justify my actions. I'm sorry, Jaden, but I'm not about to discuss why I love another man."

"That's funny because the way I remembered it you loved me."

I did, with all my heart. "Well, a funny thing about love. People have a tendency to use the words when they really don't mean it."

Jaden was quiet, but the intense expression on his face showed that his mind was working. She took a moment to think about what she had just said and realized that he probably thought she was talking about her own feelings instead of his. She sighed. No point in correcting her mistake. Instead, she'd let him see what it felt like to be hurt.

"Answer one question…did our time together mean anything to you?" He was looking at her with those dark eyes of his and suddenly she was filled with the urgent desire to kiss him.

"No! I mean, of course it did."

"Hell, I can't tell the way you just walked away and never turned back."

"Our time together meant more to me than you'll ever know," she blurted before she realized what she said.

Jaden's eyes softened. She was frozen as she watched him close the distance between them and cupped her chin. Despite the anger that still ticked at his jaw, he stared down at her, desire lurking at the corners of his mouth. "What part do you miss most?"

She swallowed hard and had sense enough not to answer his question.

"Tell me. Do you remember me making love to you? I never forgot. I still remember the way you sighed every time I filled your body."

Her stomach quivered.

"I remember the way you wrapped your legs tightly around my waist and held on while I drove even deeper," he said in a husky whisper.

She tore her gaze from his eyes and found her focus drifting lower to his mouth. She licked her lips. "Yes."

Jaden lowered his head. "Then you do remember how good we were together."

"I remember."

"So do I, which is why I have to do this."

Jaden backed her against the hood of a Honda Civic and pressed his chest and thighs to hers. Seduced by his heat and his commanding lips, Danica forgot about everything else and lost herself in the storm of Jaden's kiss. Wild and eager, their lips and tongue intertwined, each fueled by a desire buried for far too long. Need beyond anything Danica had thought possible consumed her. She wrapped her arms around his waist, holding on, needing this heat.

Arching against him, she felt the evidence of his rock-hard erection pressed against her belly. With his knee, he pushed her legs apart, wanting her to feel him.

Danica welcomed his hands beneath her skirt, his eager exploration of her thighs and hips. Desperate to re-acquaint herself with the feel of his sculpted torso, she slipped her hands beneath his T-shirt. Just as she touched his bare skin, skimming her fingers over his powerful back, Jaden's fingers slid beneath the confines of her panties. Her legs trembled when he cupped her buttocks and began an impatient massage.

Jaden tore his lips from hers. She opened her eyes to find him staring down at her. The air between them electrified. His sable eyes burned with desire. "I've missed you. I think about our time together all the time. I have for the last year."

She didn't believe him. It had all been a game. Even worse was knowing that and still wishing he really wanted her, missed her, as well. Wishing he had thought about her as often as she'd thought about him.

"Then why—" Her words were cut off by a gasp when he teased her tender flesh with his fingers, then slipped one inside. She was so hot and wet, she was ready to explode.

Thrusting her hips against his hand, she sought release. "Yes," she moaned as he kissed her face and whispered her name. Her moan rose into a cry as the rhythm of his touch increased. For countless nights she had wanted this man, yearned for his touch.

"Did it bother you seeing me with Martina?" he asked.

She stared up to find him studying her. How could she explain to him that it had bothered her when she didn't have any right to be jealous? He wasn't her man. Never had been. "Yes, but it shouldn't."

"You're right, it shouldn't because the only woman I want is you." On that note, he lowered his mouth and captured hers in another searing kiss. "Come home with me, Danica. Let me love you. Today, tonight…all night." His words clattered out in a growl.

"I can't," she said, struggling, reminding herself that Jaden wasn't doing anything but feeding her more lies.

He pulled back slightly. "At least have dinner with me and then we can see where the evening leads."

She took a moment to gaze up at him. The dark sensual look in his eyes was making her consider things she shouldn't. Already she had allowed him to do more than they should have. A sly smile curled his lips and promises of pleasure lurked in his eyes. Suddenly reality hit her like a dump truck. What in the world was she doing? This was the man who had broken her heart. Did he really think she was going to allow him to take her through that again? She wanted more than just sex. For the first time in her life, she wanted it to be about wanting and needing her heart, her love.

His mouth feathered her lips as he spoke. "I can come by your house to pick you up around eight."

Knowing them, they would never make it past the front door before they started pulling each other's clothes off. As much as she missed his touch, there was no way she was letting him take her down that road again. With one shove she pushed him away.

"I already have plans," she lied and moved away from the car.

His gaze was deep and intense. "For a moment I thought—" He caught himself, his mouth clamped shut. Jaden shook off whatever he was about to say, then looked down at his watch. "All right. If you change your mind you know where to reach me."

Yeah, right. She could just bet the wheels in his mind were churning. He probably already had another dinner date he was going to call who would guarantee his night would end beneath her sheets.

Why the hell do you care? "I guess I'll see you tomorrow."

Nodding, he turned away just as the cell phone at his hip rang. He brought it to his ear and strolled to the other side of the garage. She stood there watching, trying to ignore the solid muscles moving beneath his work clothes. Every time he came near her, every time he touched her, she yearned to taste him again. Somehow she was going to have to keep her emotions under lock and key.

His voice rumbled with laughter, breaking her from her trance. She swung on her heels, anxious to put distance between her and the shop as fast as she could.

The sun had begun to set when Jaden moved into his room and slipped out of his jeans. Staying at the garage until he was ready to drop hadn't helped at all. He was in desperate need of a cold shower, although it would do little to cure his sexual ache for Danica. Having her up underfoot day after day was starting to take its toll on him.

What the hell had he been thinking?

That was the problem, he thought with a scowl. He hadn't been thinking, at least not with the right body part. He couldn't blame anyone but himself. He was the one who insisted that she work for him in exchange for fixing her car for free so he could have her near him again. So he had no one to blame for his life being turned upside down but himself. Their past relationship should have been enough for him to want to stay far away.

Moving over to the window, he raked a hand across his locks. While staring out at the ocean, he tried to clear his head of the afternoon's events but couldn't see past the frustration. He should have known she would never admit hurting him by her lies. Did she realize how long it had taken him to work her out of his system? And for what? They never had a real relationship. All they'd ever really had was lust.

And the kind of sex a man never forgets.

After Danica had walked out on him, Jaden spent weeks feeling sorry for himself until he had finally pulled himself together and decided she wasn't worth the time or effort, and started dating. Only none of the women he encountered could hold a torch to Danica and he found himself constantly comparing them to her.

Closing his eyes, Jaden could almost taste her smooth cinnamon-colored skin sliding beneath his lips. Just thinking about her had him longing to touch and run his fingers through her massive reddish-brown curls. He had once thought the color came out of a bottle until he discovered her hair was the same color in other areas of her body. Speaking of other areas, he felt his penis throb with longing.

Shaken by the depth of his need, he moved into the bathroom and turned on the shower and immediately stripped and moved under the spray of the water. The cold temporarily cleared his mind. He hated himself for that weakness. What happened at the garage had been one big mistake. What was even worse was the fact that Danica had rejected him—again.

He stuck his head under the showerhead, rinsing the dirt from his locks. He had to get it together and face the fact. Danica was engaged to another man and nothing he said or did was going to change that. She belonged to another man and the sooner he realized that the better off he would be.

Dammit! Hiring Danica had been a big mistake. So far, all she had done was stir up feelings.

Anger.

Frustration.

And lust.

From day one the sex had been incredible, and he knew from that first moment that nothing else would ever compare. The sex between them had always been good and he had never grown tired of moving on top of her and fitting snuggly inside her.

Having her working at the shop, close to him, was not about risking his heart. It was supposed to be about getting answers and extracting her from his heart forever. All he had to do was get his hormones to cooperate.

We'll see about that.

What he needed was some quick sexual release and he knew just who to call. Desperate times call for desperate measures.

He turned off the water, then reached for a towel and moved back into his room. As soon as he took a seat on the end of the bed, he dialed the phone. It was answered on the second ring.

"Hello?" a sweet voice answered.

Jaden's lips curled with pleasure. She was one of a handful of women he'd been seeing since his return to Sheraton Beach. He and Candy went way back to their high school days. She wasn't looking for anything serious and that was just fine with him.

"Whassup, Candy?"

"Whassup with you?" she purred.

"Just getting in from the shop and was wondering if you wanted some company?" he asked in a deep seducing tone.

"I would love for you to come over. I already got your side of the bed warm."

He laughed. "I'll be over shortly."

Jaden hung up the phone, then moved to get dressed. In less than an hour, Danica would be the furthest thing from his mind.

Danica finally gave up trying to enjoy a book and tossed it aside. What was the use? She'd been reading the same paragraph for over an hour and didn't have the slightest idea what the scene was about.

Rising from the bed, she moved over to the window and stared out at the large hill over the small beach town where the Beaumont Hotel stood boldly on top. Lights from the beautiful structure were faint in the distance. There, guests ate meals cooked by chefs from all around the country and slept beneath sheets with more thread than she could even count. There were three pools, a golf course, tennis, a gym with personal trainers and a private beach. The hotel was a world of its own. With boutiques occupying the entire lobby, guests didn't have to go out for anything because everything they could ever want was right at their fingertips.

She nibbled on her lips as she remembered Jaden talking about growing up spending every weekend working on the hotel floors, learning the ins and outs of the corporation. Even as far back as the fifth grade, he knew the hotel industry was not his cup of tea. Instead he wanted to follow his dream. His stubborn determination was what she had loved about him. She frowned. It was also part of the reason why she couldn't stop thinking about him. As crazy as it was, she wished more than anything she had joined him for dinner tonight. Just being able to sit across the table from him and watch his lips while he ate would be all the satisfaction she needed. What harm would there have been in simply eating?

Everything and you know it.

She heaved a heavy breath and moved away from the window. She had made the right choice. Going out with him would have been setting herself up for failure. It was bad enough she couldn't get their kisses off her mind. A part of her regretted what had happened, but another part was yearning for a lot more. She hadn't had time for sex, but that man reminded her that she was long overdue. A moan escaped her lips. Jaden knew about passion. How to stir it. How to savor it. He had been a wonderful lover, which was why she needed to stay clear of him. No matter how much she missed him.

Gosh, you're pathetic.

What she needed was someone to talk to. Before she had a chance to think about what she was doing, she was dialing the phone and hearing her sister's voice come over the line.

"Something must be wrong if you're calling me."

"Why do you say that?" Danica asked with a soft chuckle.

"Because I'm the one who's always doing the calling. The only time you call is if you want something or if something is bothering you," she added, rushing on. "So what's the problem, chickadee?"

She smiled. Maureen hadn't called her that in years. "I'm starting to think that I might be in over my head with my new boss."

"As in *new* boss, you must be talking about Jason."

"It's Jaden and yes, I'm talking about him." She swung her legs over the side of the bed and moved toward the kitchen.

"Is it getting too hot for you to handle?"

She paused at the top step. "Yes, how did you know?"

"Girl, puhleeze. You and him all alone in an auto body shop. I can imagine quite a few things happening on the hood of a car."

Danica almost stumbled on the last step. How was it her sister always knew what was going on? "I almost gave him some this afternoon."

"Almost? What's wrong with you? You should be telling me you *did* give him some."

Danica removed a mug from the cabinet and filled it with water. "I don't want to go through that again. I want him to want more than sex."

"What's wrong with sex?"

"Nothing, but you know I have a hard time separating my heart from my body," she said as she put the mug in the microwave and turned it on. Tea with honey and lemon was just what she needed to ease her mind.

"Are you still in love with him?"

The question was met by a moment of silence as she tried to think about her answer. "If you had asked me that a week ago I would have said no, but now I'm not so sure."

"Then it's probably a good thing that you stay away."

"What? Maureen's telling me to pass on the sex. Is this really my big sister on the other end?"

"I'm serious. I don't want to see you get hurt."

"Neither do I. I thought I was over him but I'm not."

"How does he feel about you?"

"He told me he missed me and never stopped thinking about me, but I don't believe him."

"Maybe there's some truth that might be worth exploring."

The microwave timer went off. She opened its door with a heavy sigh of despair. "I don't think so. The sooner he fixes my car, the better off we'll both be."

"All I want is for you to be happy. Remember when we were kids and we used to watch Mama and Daddy kissing?"

Danica reached inside the refrigerator and retrieved a lemon. "Yep, it always made me feel warm inside. They were so in love."

"Yes, they were."

Forty years of marriage. That's what she wanted, to grow old together with the man she loved. To be happy the way her parents were. She released a heavy sigh. "That's what I want and I'm not settling for anything less."

"Then go for what you stand for."

Her sister always knew what to say. "I love you, Maureen."

"I love you, too, chickadee."

Jaden pulled up in front of Candy's ranch-style home and put his SUV in park, but found he was in no rush to get out. On the entire ride over, all he could think about was Danica.

"Damn," he said. Just thinking about Danica sent a jolt through him that traveled straight down to his midsection.

Why did she have to come back into his life now?

He closed his eyes and could smell her. That subtle scent of flowers and amber. The same scent that always reminded him of Danica. And anytime he smelled it, out on the street, he found himself turning around expecting to see her standing somewhere close by.

Dammit, he couldn't do it. Jaden was about to call off the evening because he couldn't make himself get out of the car. He knew the last person he wanted to be with was Candy. Not when the only person he wanted to be with was trying to drive him crazy.

His phone rang and he looked down and cursed under his breath when Candy's number displayed.

"Why are you sitting out there? The door's open," she purred.

He took a deep breath. "Candy, I can't do this. I'm sorry."

There was a long pause before Candy finally asked, "So, who is she?"

"Who is who?"

Candy laughed. "The woman who has your heart." At his silence she continued. "Whoever she is, tell her she's one lucky woman."

Chapter 8

On Thursday Jaden pulled his Denali onto a redbrick driveway in front of Beaumont Manor and killed the engine. Cars lined the semicircle, signifying that everyone was already here. Glancing down at his watch, he groaned.

Mother is going to kill me.

He was over an hour later for dinner. The family was probably already eating dessert. But being late couldn't be helped.

After last night, he decided that the sooner he got Danica's Mercedes running and a receptionist hired the better. Then he could go back to life the way it was. At closing time, he had removed the engine from Danica's car and got started and somehow lost track of time. And now he was late.

Jaden climbed out and took a moment to gaze over

at the huge two-story brick home on five acres of plush green land, overlooking the ocean that ran along the right of the property. This was the home he had grown up in and the same place he ran from the second he graduated from high school. Money and prestige, being a member of the elite class of African Americans in the state of Delaware had never meant anything of importance to him. In fact, being a Beaumont had often left him feeling uncomfortable because people judged him for what he had been instead of the man he had become. That was one of the reasons why he had left to find who he really was without his parents pressuring him to join all the others at the Beaumont Hotel. His decision caused a rift between him and his parents, and for years he and his father seldom spoke, but he was pleased to know that since his return he and his father had come to a better understanding and had resolved their differences.

Jaden moved onto a long porch that dominated the front, where his younger sister, Bianca, was relaxed in one of the wicker chairs drinking lemonade.

"It's about time!" The nutmeg beauty sprang from the seat and launched herself at him. Pulling back slightly, she gave him a long scolding look. "We thought you weren't coming. Mother was having a hissy fit."

"I got sidetracked."

Leaning closer, Jaden kissed his sister's silken cheek, her sweet perfume lingering in his nostrils. At twenty-four, Bianca could be overly dramatic at times. She had inherited that trait from their mother. He glanced down at her short brown hair, cut to fall in layers, and wide walnut eyes that sparkled with excitement.

"By who?" she asked inquisitively.

"More like what."

"If it's a *what,* then you must be talking about a car." Shaking her head, she looped her arm through his and steered him into the soaring, two-story foyer.

"Well, you'll be pleased to hear that Stephanie and her grandmother left about fifteen minutes ago. She stuck her pointy nose in the air and announced, 'I don't wait for anyone!' and stormed out of the house."

A smile curled his lips at his sister's impersonation of the bougie woman. "Really?"

Bianca gave his shoulder a playful punch. "Don't try to act all innocent. We both know that's the reason why you're late."

"No, but it's definitely a wonderful bonus." He laughed, and Bianca joined in.

They strolled across gleaming oak hardwood floors past the gallery of photographed Beaumonts, several generations that adorned the walls, and to the left of a double staircase they entered the family room.

Jace and Jabarie were standing at the bar with their father, Roger Beaumont. His sisters-in-law, Sheyna and Brenna, were sitting on a red-velvet couch across from his mother, who was holding his niece Arianna. As soon as they moved through the door, all eyes were on him.

Bianca tossed her long acrylic nails through the air. "Mother, look who finally wandered through the door!"

"Thanks, I thought you were on my side," Jaden mumbled close to Bianca's ear. Giggling, she jumped out of his reach and moved to her niece, who was holding out her arms.

His mother rose and gave him a scolding look that told him he was in for an earful later.

He gave her an innocent look. "Sorry, Mother. I lost track of time."

She gave him a pretty pout. "I guess spending time with your family isn't important to you."

He groaned under his breath. She was going to try and make him feel guilty.

"Let me go and have them put dinner on the table. Hopefully it isn't ruined." She moved over and he planted a kiss on her smooth cheek before she left the room.

His father signaled for him to come and join him. "Son, come on over and have a drink with us."

He met the three smiling faces and took the glass of bourbon from his father's hand. "Thanks." His father reached out and embraced him in a bear hug. It amazed him how family had finally become important to a man who at one time nothing meant more to him than his hotel chain. Now the workaholic couldn't get enough of being a grandfather and called his children on the phone at least once a week.

Jabarie moved around and patted him on his back. "Your future wife and her mama just left."

"Good," he replied, then tilted the glass. The men chuckled openly.

"What are you all laughing about?" Brenna asked inquisitively from across the room. "Don't tell me my husband is misbehaving."

"Why does it have to be me?" Jabarie asked innocently.

She rose and came around to join them. "Because I know you." She moved up to him and placed a kiss on his lips.

Jabarie had to resist a grin.

Bianca came over carrying his niece. He kissed her

cheek and stared down at her precious little face. She had beautiful caramel skin like her mother and the Beaumonts' sable-brown eyes. She was going to be a heartbreaker. Jabarie was going to have his hands full keeping the boys away.

"I heard you're working on Danica's car?" he heard Bianca ask, and then the room got quiet.

He took another sip. "Yes, I'm working on her car."

His father looked from one to the other with a puzzled look. "Who's Danica?"

"The one Jaden let get away," Bianca teased. He gave her a warning but she ignored him. "She had his nose wide open there for a second."

"She sure did," Brenna cosigned.

He moved behind the bar and poured himself another drink. With a room filled with women, he knew he was in trouble.

"And she's working with him at the shop," Sheyna added as she came over to join in on the fun.

He had a feeling he could thank Jace for providing her with that piece of information.

"So are you going to work things out with her?" Sheyna asked.

"Yeah, are you?" Brenna repeated.

Jaden shook his head, amused by their interrogation. "Ladies, not that it's any of your business, Danica ended our relationship, not me."

Sheyna looked from one woman to the other and frowned. "That's not what she told me."

He took a sip before he replied, "Then you need to ask her again. She ended our relationship because she's engaged to someone else."

The room grew quiet again and suddenly the

women roared with laughter. The men exchanged confused looks.

"What's so funny?" Jace finally asked.

Sheyna waved her hand in the air. "Danica isn't engaged. That's just an excuse."

Jaden glared over the rim of his glass. "Excuse? What do you mean, she isn't engaged?"

Sheyna's eyes sparkled with laughter. "All the time I've known her she has never once mentioned a fiancé. She's talks about men, even been dating, but never once has she mentioned a fiancé."

There was no way she could have been lying. "Then who was that guy at your wedding?"

She shrugged. "A date."

Why did he think that was her fiancé?

He must have had a puzzled look on his face because Sheyna started laughing again. "Come on, Jaden, haven't you noticed she isn't wearing an engagement ring?"

Brenna snorted rudely. "Yep, that would do it."

He *had* noticed that she wasn't wearing a ring, but he figured it was because she was too busy messing around to remember to put it on. But then he hadn't seen one the other day or the day before that, either. "She's not engaged. Believe me, I know her well enough. Ask her nicely. I'm sure she'll tell you the truth."

The women were still laughing when their mother came to signal them it was time for dinner.

All during dinner, Jaden was quiet as he thought about what Sheyna had told him. Was he that blind that he didn't see the signs?

After dinner he went to the bar in the great room and poured himself another drink.

"So," Jace asked, filling his glass with bourbon,

"now that you know the truth, what are you going to do about you and Danica?"

"Find out the truth," Jaden answered. Yes, he was going to get answers once and for all.

A new challenge filled him. He had a mission. Places in his soul that he hadn't known were empty suddenly overflowed with anticipation.

"Well," Jabarie chuckled. "I wouldn't believe it if I hadn't seen it with my own eyes."

Jaden frowned at him. "What's that?"

"You, being crazy about something other than an automobile."

"I'm not going to lie," he answered. "I'm crazy about Danica, even loved her once." *And probably still do.*

There was a beat of silence before Jace asked, "How does she feel about you?"

"I don't know," he answered, "but I plan to find out."

He was determined to find out why she had lied to him and show her how good they were together if it was the last thing he did.

Chapter 9

"Kyle said you wanted to see me."

At the sound of her voice, soft and uncertain, Jaden glanced up from his sandwich to find Danica standing in the doorway of his office. She looked into his eyes and he felt sucker punched in the gut. No other woman affected him that way. Only Danica. It was her scent that hit him next. Something that reminded him of a tropical location where lemons and oranges grew wild. The scent made him want to scoop her up into his arms and carry her to the bed in back and do what he'd been dying to do for days. And now that he knew she wasn't engaged, he had every intention of satisfying his sexual craving. It might take weeks or months but he had to have her again.

He had been avoiding her all morning waiting for the time to get her alone and had asked Tim and Kyle on their way out to lunch to ask Danica to come back to see him.

While he chewed he took a moment to take in the short gray skort and white blouse. Her long legs were bare and her white flat sandals left her pink-painted toes exposed.

"Did you hear what I said?"

Danica's question invaded his thoughts and he tipped his head and met her eyes. "Yes, I heard you. I just wanted to let you know the parts for your engine should be here tomorrow."

Clearly pleased, Danica pushed away from the door and lowered herself onto the chair across from him with a heavy breath. "That's good news. How long do you think it's going to take for you to fix it?"

"As busy as it's been around here, probably a week or two." Or even longer if he could help it. He wasn't ready yet to part from seeing her beautiful face every morning, not until he got answers.

She nodded. "That sounds wonderful. I'm tired of being without transportation."

A tinge of guilt hit him. It hadn't occurred to him that without her Mercedes she was handicapped. "I have a Honda Civic around back that you're more than welcome to use."

Her shoulders sagged noticeably with relief. "That would be wonderful."

Jaden reached into his pocket and removed his keys and slipped off the Honda key. Leaning across the table, he handed it to her.

"Thanks," she said with a smile. "I need to buy groceries this weekend and hated to have to get a cab."

"No problem," he said with a wink. "I'm sorry that I hadn't thought of it sooner. Besides, you could have called me. I would have been more than happy to have taken you wherever you needed to go." He gave her an intense look as he dropped his elbows onto the table and leaned forward.

Suddenly Danica's smile faded and she looked almost uncomfortable. After clearing her throat, she replied, "I got those parts ordered that you needed for Charlene's Camry. I think I called every auto parts store in the state, but they should be here first thing in the morning."

Jaden reached for his sandwich and said between chews, "She'll be glad to hear that, although my best advice for Charlene is to get rid of that money pit. Every time I fix that car something else goes wrong, but she refused to listen to me." The 1990 four-door sedan had seen better days.

Danica smiled. "I'm sure you were the same way with your first car. I know I was."

He had to chuckle at the memories. "Mine was a 1978 Cutlass Supreme. I drove that sucker until the bottom fell out."

This time she laughed, chuckled really, the sound full and honest, but when his eyes met hers, she quickly sobered. It was Danica who decided to get things back to professional. "I have two interviews scheduled for you for tomorrow and another on Tuesday."

"Okay," he began with a nod. He noticed she seemed a little on edge, so he decided to change the subject. "How was your weekend?"

She stared at him for several longs seconds with her eyes narrowed almost as if she didn't trust him before her shoulders relaxed and she gave a slight shrug. "The contractor came in and started building the dressing rooms. If I had known there was going to be sawdust all over the place I would have waited to order my inventory."

"Yeah, it can get a bit messy," Jaden replied and focused on her mouth as she continued to speak passionately about her boutique.

Unlike her, Jaden had spent the weekend thinking about Danica and trying to figure out why she would lie about being engaged. He could have kicked himself because the truth was so obvious. She wasn't wearing a ring. Not because she was trying to open a boutique, but because there was no ring to begin with. If he hadn't been so bitter about her ending their relationship, he would have discovered her explanation was fishy from the get go.

Watching her lips, he became obsessed with finding out the truth. Jaden realized he wasn't going to be able to last another minute until he got an answer, so he decided to come out and ask her one question and see how she reacted.

"I'm curious…" he began between chews. "What's your fiancé's name?"

From the look on her face, Jaden knew his question caught her totally off guard. "Uh…Kenyon," she stuttered.

"Really?" he replied between chews. "Kenyon what?"

"Kenyon Clark."

He gave her an intent look. "How did the two of you meet?"

Danica frowned, her ruby-red lips forming a luscious pout. "Why are you suddenly so interested in my personal life?"

He gave her a simple shrug. "It's good to always know who your competition is."

Her eyes flickered with surprise and this time the

suspicion was apparent. "Competition? There's no competition, because there's nothing going on between us."

Jaden purposely hesitated as if he was giving her comment consideration. "Okay. But since we're working together can we at least try to be friends?"

His question was met by a skeptical look before she finally said, "Sure."

"Good." He reached for his soda and took a thirsty swallow. "So have you and *Kenyon* at least set a wedding date?"

The line of questioning was evidently making her nervous, because she was playing with her hands. "Um, next summer."

He nodded. "They say summer is a busy time."

"So they say."

"When do we get a chance to meet your fiancé?"

Her brow rose. "Who is *we?*"

"Your friends here in Sheraton Beach. I would like a chance to see if he's worthy of you. Obviously, I wasn't the right man for the job, otherwise, you wouldn't have ended our relationship." He paused long enough to bring the can to his lips. "Because I care about you, I want to make sure he's the right man for you."

Danica shot him a straight no-nonsense look. "How would *you* know what that is?"

"Because I do. You're a beautiful, sweet, compassionate woman, and you deserve a good man. Not some brotha who can't look past the legendary model."

Danica couldn't resist a grin. "I'm far from legendary."

He smiled. "Tell that to someone else. I have a copy of every magazine you were ever in."

"No, you don't," she replied and shook her head with disbelief.

"Yes, I do," Jaden said as he put the soda can down. "Come to my place and I'll show you."

He studied her face for a moment, her expression not quite a frown, and noticed Danica started nibbling nervously on her bottom lip. What was it about her mouth that made it so desirable? *Kissable.* Her lips were full and succulent and positively suckable. He wanted more than anything to kiss her, wanted to drink her in while he explored her body with his hands.

"I don't think so," she finally said.

Jaden moved out of his chair and came around to the other side of the desk. "Why, what are you afraid of?"

She barely stopped herself from rolling her eyes. "I'm not afraid of anything."

The rational part of Danica's mind told her Jaden was up to something. But her body wasn't paying her brain any attention as she found herself rising from the chair. "If you'll excuse me, I need to get to the boutique and finish ordering inventory." Before she did something stupid, she turned and moved toward the door.

Jaden shot after her and grabbed her arm, pulling until she turned to face him. "Why the rush?"

She was breathless, startled and the pulse at her throat hammered frantically. "I've got a business to open."

"A few more minutes won't make that much of a difference. I want to finish talking about your fiancé." He raised a hand to her cheek. "But first I need to talk about the way you make me feel."

Danica's heart pounded. Her mind raced. She was almost sure her knees were going to give out. Jaden ran

his fingers along her face and neck while smiling down
at her as though he knew something she didn't.

"What do you mean, how *I* make you feel?"

"I can't stop thinking about how good you taste." He
licked his lips, then gave her a disarming smile. She knew
there was so much behind that smile. Jaden was used to
getting whatever her wanted or needed. Hunger burned
in his eyes as he slid a finger across her bottom lip.

"What…what are you doing?" she asked.

He moved forward. "Getting ready to kiss you."

Now was not the time to give in to her emotions.
Concentrate. Danica drew in a deep breath and let it out.
Scraping up what strength she had left, she wrenched
herself away from his touch, backing up until she met
his large desk. "Why?"

"Because I need to taste you again."

There was nothing she could do to block her body's
instant response to him. Her pulse was beating heavily
while desire raced hot and hard inside her.

What stopped her from voicing her yearning was the
fear that if she tasted him again, this time she might not
want him to stop. Danica knew she should tell him no
and insist that he let her go, but she couldn't get the
words to form and instead of pulling away, she dipped
her head slightly.

He closed the little distance that was left between
them and cupped her face. "Danica, look at me."

Chin up, Danica drew in a deep breath. Meeting his
gaze, she witnessed the desire burning in his eyes. Her
stomach quivered. No other man tempted her that way.
Only Jaden.

Another tremor moved through her. "I don't think
kissing me is a good idea."

"I think it is." Jaden brushed his mouth across hers and pressed his warm body against her. "Kiss me, Danica."

"No." She fought against her own shameful weakness to him. Danica found herself trembling inside, the thrill of anticipation doubling her pulse.

"You know you want me to kiss you," he said, moving his hand to run his fingers along her side, just barely grazing the side of her breast.

"No, I don't." She tried to lie to herself that she didn't want him, but her traitorous body wasn't listening.

"Yes, you do. Go ahead and tell me…tell me to kiss you."

She stared down at his lips and found she couldn't resist. She didn't want to. This was what her body had been craving all weekend. Their eyes locked.

"You're right. I want you to kiss me," she whispered hoarsely.

Jaden slanted his mouth over hers and rewarded her with a long slow kiss that tore a whimper from her throat.

He pulled her closer and, reaching down, slid his hand beneath her skirt, up her thigh and his fingers brushed the triangle of curls. She gasped, breaking the kiss by turning her head. She cursed him under her breath yet she hesitated to stop his wandering hand.

Cupping her chin, Jaden brought her mouth back to his. Her lips parted and he slipped his tongue inside, tasting her with a finesse that sent heat straight down between her thighs. Gasping, she could do nothing but cling to him, forgetting all the reasons why giving in to her emotions was wrong.

The skirt bunched easily at her waist, exposing her satin panties. Heat raced through her and her cheeks flamed. What in the world was she doing? She was leaned back against Jaden's desk; her skirt was up around her waist. He pushed her thighs apart, and with him standing between her legs, she could feel what she yearned to have inside her. A soft cry escaped her and she arched toward him. She wanted to hold him, wrap her legs around him and take him inside.

Danica knew she should tell him to let her go. After all, her heart was supposed to belong to another man. But she was on fire, and instead, she allowed her head to fall back as his mouth moved to her throat. It was as if her body had taken over. No other man had ever made her feel this alive. And not just any man. "Jaden," she murmured. "Oh, Jaden."

The touch of his mouth sent wildfire racing under skin. Her hips arched against him. Her body had responded all too well to him. Not only that, but he had responded, as well. With her body aligned with his, she could feel the pressure of his growing erection pressed against where her body wanted him.

Jaden's hands stroked over her face and down her arms. What he did next almost made her knees buckle. He curled his hand around her breast and stroked his thumb over the material that separated him from the hard, swollen surface of her nipple. It was sheer torture. She was on fire. Her entire body shuddered with it.

"You're driving me crazy," she whispered.

"Good." His voice was a deep, throaty growl.

Their hips were anchored together by the fierce tug of desire between them. Instead of backing off, he drew closer again and caressed the curve of her bottom.

She groaned softly when his lips whispered over hers, gently, inquisitively. She felt his breath mingling with hers, the scent of his cologne and his keen maleness engulfing her. Yearning bit deep into her core. She responded without thought, driven by desire, reaching to press her mouth firmly to his.

He took the offering, kissing her deeply, mastering her senses in an instant. He explored her lower lip as if he were claiming it as his territory. While his tongue tasted hers, one strong hand moved over the surface of her breast with deliberation.

Needing to feel him, she slipped her hands underneath his T-shirt and trailed her fingers along his back. Firm muscle flexed at her touch. His sudden intake of breath nearly stole hers. He was growing harder by the second, and she wanted to touch it, wanted to feel it in her hand, wanted to feel it thrusting deep inside her.

He lowered her blouse and held the weight of her high breasts in his big hands, cupping and thumbing her taut nipples. He kissed her while he rolled her sensitive peaks between his thumb and forefinger.

"I'm going to taste you here," he murmured as he took one swollen nipple into his mouth, then the other. Stunned by his boldness, she could barely form a rational thought. Jaden moved his tongue wickedly, then plucked at her nipple with one hand while he licked and nibbled her other breast. There was no urgency in his foreplay. He was all about taking his long torturous time and was scratching at every nerve in her body.

Danica lost her will to fight, as she moaned and arched toward his mouth, offering herself to him. She couldn't stop now even if she wanted to. He captured the other nipple between his teeth and flicked his tongue over the very end, while she whimpered. His tongue swirled and lapped and Danica strained to thrust more and more of her breast into his mouth.

"Hey, Jaden! You back here? I brought you some gumbo just the way you like it, hot and spicy."

The low throaty rasp of a woman's voice startled Danica. She broke off the kiss and pulled her blouse closed just as a beautiful woman with long flowing curls and beautiful buttercream skin came through the door. In a flowery bikini covered only by a hip sarong the woman held a picnic basket. She stopped short at the door when she discovered Jaden wasn't alone in his office. "Oh, Jaden, I'm sorry. I thought you were over here working too hard, so I thought I'd bring you over some of Mama's cooking. But I see you're occupied," she said casually. "I'll just leave this here for you." She set the basket on the table.

"Thanks, Diane, I appreciate it." He winked at her and smiled. "It'll definitely get eaten for dinner."

"And I can see you're in the middle of lunch," she said, taking a quick glance at Danica.

With an apologetic smile, Jaden released Danica, then stepped outside the office door with Diane and exchanged a few words. Danica watched him shake his head when she whispered something throaty and inviting near his ear. Reality struck her like a glass of ice water. What in the world was she doing practically making love on the desk with a man who was only capable of breaking her heart? Apparently Diane was just another woman on his list despite everything he said about missing and wanting her back in his life.

"Don't work too hard," Danica heard Diane say followed by a giggle before moving across the garage and exiting through the reception area.

When Jaden finally stepped back into the office with a silly smirk on his face, everything became clear. A few moments ago, she had lost her head by allowing herself to remember what it had once been like with Jaden, the man she had given herself unconditionally to. Suddenly, she felt foolish and stupid for pretending that nothing had changed, when, actually, everything had.

Feeling like a fool, Danica tried to brush past him to get away, but he was like a block of granite, too strong to move. He reached for her arms and held her without budging. When she glared into his eyes, he shrugged and said calmly, "She's a friend."

Danica wasn't a fool. She doubted Jaden had female "friends" who brought him lunch in a bikini. She shook her head. "I think I'd better go."

"I don't want you to leave. Stay and share the lunch. I'm certain Diane made more than enough for two."

"That's because she planned to share it with you. If you hurry you might be able to catch her. Now if you'll excuse me." Danica's voice was deliberately rich with sarcasm.

"I don't want to eat with her. I want to eat you, if you'll let me," he shot back with a playful grin.

Danica ignored the sizzle at her middle. "I don't think so." His kiss had stolen her breath, but she had regained normal breathing. "In fact, let me go and catch her for you."

Jaden pursed his lips. "Danica, do you really think it's that easy for me to switch partners. I was just trying to make love to you. Do you really think there's a voice in my head that says 'switch' as the next woman comes along?"

"I don't know what goes through your mind. All I know is that I'm engaged, and this is a mistake."

Releasing her, he raked a frustrated hand across his locks. "Listen, maybe I was out of line a few minutes ago. But I'm not going to lie, now that I've tasted you again it's not going to be easy staying away from you."

His words caused her to quiver and she forced herself to swallow. "I'll admit I was wrong for allowing you to keep kissing me, but if we're going to continue to work together from this point on we need to keep it strictly business."

His lips thinned. "If that's what you want?"

"Yes, it is." She stood her ground and kept her focus on his unflinching face.

Finally Jaden nodded. "I won't do anything you don't want me to do."

Danica drew in a deep breath, wondering how she would continue to work with the only man who could anger her and make her yearn terribly for his touch at the same time.

"I'll see you tomorrow." She turned on her heels and moved back to her desk, reached for her purse and headed out toward the beach.

The chemistry between them was stronger than ever. Kissing Jaden, almost letting him make love to her on his desk was enough to tell Danica her feelings for him went deeper than their months apart could erase.

I won't do anything you don't want me to do.

Great, she thought ruefully. She'd just realized that Jaden hadn't agreed to her terms at all, but instead, he had issued her a challenge.

"Yo, Jaden, man, come on. It's your turn."

Jaden brought the bottle to his lips and finished the beer in one large swallow. Rising, he reached for his bowling ball and moved to the end of the aisle. He took a deep breath and let the ball go down the lane. *Another gutter ball.*

"What the hell is wrong with you?" Jabarie barked.

"I'm having a bad night."

"Obviously."

Rolling his eyes, Jaden went back to drinking another beer under the dim lights in the bowling alley and watched as Jace bowl another strike.

"Now, that's how you bowl!" Jabarie cried.

"I know that's right. Not all of us are on our game tonight," Jace said, adding more salt to his wound.

Jaden glared over at the two of them, then brought the bottle to his lips. They were right. He wasn't himself tonight and knew the reason was that he couldn't get Danica off his mind.

If he hadn't known it before he definitely knew it now, Danica wasn't engaged. If it had been someone else it would have been funny. But no matter whether she was engaged or not, the truth of the matter was she had dumped him. It had been one thing to think she left him for another man, but it was worse now to think that she dumped him because she just didn't want to be with him. Only his pride refused to consider that possibility.

He truly believed that Danica had once loved him just as he had loved her but something had scared her and forced Danica to create a crazy last-minute story about being engaged. Instead of feeling rejected and letting his stubborn pride get the best of him eighteen months ago, he should have fought for their love.

"Man, get your head out of the sand. Marisa's staring you down."

He followed the direction of Jace's eyes and sure

enough as soon as his gaze traveled four lanes down, Marisa waved in his direction. Jaden nodded his head in acknowledgment, not wanting to be rude, then returned his attention to their table.

"Yo, man. What's gotten into you? I thought you were trying to holla at Marisa?" his cousin Diamere said, sitting down beside him with a bottle of beer in his hand.

That was before Danica showed up at the garage.

"He's too busy thinking about someone else," Jabarie replied as he dropped down on the seat across from him.

Diamere shook his head. "Man, please don't tell me you've fallen in love like these two fools here."

Jaden took a sip from his bottle, then said with a scowl, "No way."

Diamere gave a loud sigh of relief. "Thank goodness! You scared me there for a moment. You're the only one I got left to hang out with."

Jabarie snorted in response. "Just because I'm married doesn't mean I can't hang out. It just means I have someone at home waiting for me."

Diamere crossed his fingers as if he were trying to keep the vampires away. "Like I said I don't want any part of that."

"You weren't saying that when Ryan was trying to put those twins on you."

Diamere scowled at the reminder. "That's because I was trying to do right by her. You see what I did the second I found out the truth, I headed straight for divorce court."

Jaden shook his head even though he understood why his cousin was bitter. Diamere had ended a relationship with a woman he had loved because his ex-girlfriend swore she was pregnant with his twins. Not wanting his kids to grow up without a father, he ended the relationship and married Ryan. The marriage was rocky from the start but he was willing to hang in there. His sons were barely a year old when a man came onto his job claiming to be the twins' natural father. A blood test confirmed he was right. By the time Diamere divorced Ryan, the woman he loved had married someone else.

Diamere lowered his beer bottle, curious. "Who's this honey that's got him all strung out?"

Jace leaned back on the bench and grinned as he replied, "This former swimsuit model."

"Model. You dating a model?" Diamere asked in disbelief.

Jabarie retorted, "*Was* is the operative word. She retired from modeling and is living right here in Sheraton Beach."

"No lie? A swimsuit model living in this little town?" Diamere leaned forward and gave him a devilish smile. "Yo, since you don't want her, can I have her phone number so I can show her what it's like to be with a real man."

It took everything he had not to hit his cousin in the mouth.

"Diamere, man, you better chill," Jace warned. "Jaden won't admit it but he's never gotten over that one."

"If you could see her, you'd understand why." Jabarie smiled, shaking his head.

"If she's a model, then I know she's fine." Diamere ended with a wolf whistle. "Damn, how can I get to be that lucky?"

Under normal circumstances he would have been

pissed off right about now, but from experience Jaden knew the three of them could act pretty juvenile when they all got together.

Ignoring them, he allowed his eyes to travel over to Marisa. It was her turn to bowl. He watched her throw the ball down the lane with skill and grace, sending five pins crashing down. As she swung around their eyes collided and she smiled invitingly. Jaden gave her body a once-over from the spaghetti-strap top that held her large breasts firmly in place to the tight-fitting jeans. She was a voluptuous woman, but her curves in no way compared to Danica's lush hips and thighs. Her high breasts. That woman is definitely a piece of work. *And she's driving me crazy.*

What he needed was a distraction, but he couldn't bring himself to even move over in Marisa's direction. His loins were on fire, but the only woman capable of satisfying his craving was Danica. His body refused to settle for anything else.

"I'll take that loan in small bills." Diamere's words trampled his thoughts.

Jaden turned his attention back to the table. "What did you say?"

Jabarie cut his eyes as he took a swig of his beer. "You just agreed to loan this fool twenty-five thousand dollars. And he wants it in small bills."

Jaden made a face. "Yeah, right. You still owe me from the last loan."

"And you know I'm good for it," Diamere said as he set his empty beer bottle down on the table.

He couldn't argue. When his ailing father was in danger of losing his restaurant, Diamere had come to his cousins for help. Instead of giving him a loan, Jace,

Jabarie and Jaden decided to become silent partners. Jaden was just giving Diamere a hard time. After two years, the restaurant was doing quite well.

"So, when can I meet Ms. Swimsuit Model?" his cousin asked as he reached for a plate of hot wings.

"Never," Jaden growled.

Jace leaned forward on the chair and chuckled. "Actually she's working at the garage with him in the morning. The only way he could get the woman's attention was by holding her car ransom."

Jaden tilted his glass while the men roared with laughter. "Are we going to finish bowling or what?"

"Yeah, yeah, I'm going." Diamere rose and eyed a slender woman walking by as he moved over to retrieve his ball.

Jaden took a final swig and pushed the bottle across the table. They could laugh all they wanted, but he wasn't giving up that easily. Danica was trying to act as though she didn't want him, but the body couldn't lie. If it took the entire summer, he was going to have her wet, frantic and withering beneath him again.

Chapter 10

Danica dropped her purse on the floor of her bedroom, then sank down on the bed.

I did it.

She'd survived another afternoon with Jaden without climbing onto his lap and begging him to make love to her. She was going to have to buy some loose-fitting shirts because every time he passed her she felt her nipples tighten painfully.

"This is ridiculous!" she screamed.

Thank goodness Jaden was cranky this afternoon. If he'd been charming and attentive the way he had been yesterday before Diane arrived with lunch, she would never have been able to sustain what little control she had left.

Rising, she slipped out of her slacks and knit shirt and walked around in a sports bra and panties. She had spent the afternoon and well into the evening at the boutique. It was the only way she could occupy her mind, otherwise, she'd be sitting around thinking about Jaden.

The dressing rooms were coming along. By Friday the mirrors would be up on the walls. If she kept up the pace, she would make the Memorial Day weekend celebration.

Glancing over at her clock, Danica noticed she had thirty minutes before *Law & Order Special Victim's Unit,* her favorite show. That gave her just enough time to shower, lay out clothes for tomorrow and pop in a microwave dinner.

At ten minutes to nine, she settled on the couch, reached for the remote control and turned the television to NBC. As soon as she dragged a throw cover across her legs, there was a knock at the door. She crossed the room and looked through the peephole. It was Jaden.

Great. Just great. What in the world was he doing here? Seeing him at Peterson's Garage was difficult enough. Taking a deep breath, Danica opened the door, took one look at him and felt as though she were hyperventilating. Lord, have mercy! He looked handsome standing there in khaki shorts and a wife beater.

Jaden leaned easily on the jamb, his arms crossed. "Hey," he said with a charming smile.

Her breath caught in her throat. "Hey." Jaden smelled so good. She knew he'd just showered, because his clothes were clean and he smelled so fresh, she wanted to bury her face against his neck and breathe.

His eyes traveled over her slowly. "You're in your pajamas," he said in a soft tone of surprise, as though he expected her to be wearing a skirt and high heels.

Danica glanced down at her pink pajama top and

bottoms. "That's usually what people wear to bed," she said with intentional sarcasm.

He glanced down at his watch. "Going to bed this soon?"

"No. I'm getting ready to watch television."

His eyes sparkled with interest. "Oh yeah? What are you watching?"

"Law & Order."

Jaden's boyish grin made her bones melt. *"Law & Order?"*

She nodded with a smile.

"I saw the previews this morning. This is supposed to be a new episode."

"Yes, it is." There was a long silence. "Why are you here?"

He gave an innocent shrug. "I was just in the neighborhood."

Danica didn't believe that for a second.

There was another silence before she heard him say, "Can I join you?"

No way am I going to sit through a TV program with you. That would be just too damn close for comfort. The farther away from Jaden the better, yet she couldn't seem to get her lips to cooperate. What was supposed to be a refusal came out sounding like "Sure." Next thing she knew, she had stepped back so he could enter.

As the show's teaser scene came on, Jaden settled on the couch, while Danica sat, cross-legged, on the end. When the opening theme began, she looked to her left and said, "No talking."

"Then be quiet," he shot back.

Danica playfully stuck out her tongue and noticed the exact moment his expression changed. His eyes crinkled with a slow smile, his lashes dropping over a glance that acknowledged her slip.

"Keep doing that and I'll show you exactly what to do with that tongue."

Yearning vibrated through her. Thank goodness the program started. She turned back to the television, hugging her knees protectively against her breasts. If they were going to keep things strictly professional between them, then she was going to have to watch what she said around him. It was bad enough she was sitting on the couch in pajamas. What made matters worse was that Jaden was so close, she could almost smell the fabric softener he used in his laundry mixed with his utterly distracting cologne.

Danica curled her legs beneath her and settled deeper into the corner of the couch. She managed to get through the rest of the hour by concentrating on the show and that was no easy task. She couldn't talk, had a hard time breathing because Jaden was too damn close to her. Fortunately for her, the episode gave her something else to think about besides the man sitting beside her. She waited until the ten o'clock news came on before she spoke. "That was a good episode."

Jaden nodded in agreement. "I love the way they pull issues from the headlines into each episode." His voice was a slow caress.

"Me, too," she whispered with her throat dry.

He stretched his bare legs out in front of him and raised his arms over his head. She noticed the way the material lay smugly across his chest and she itched to touch him there.

When a commercial came on, Jaden rose from the couch, but instead of heading toward the door, he moved over toward the mantel and gazed at the framed photographs of her family that lined it. While he was distracted, she took the opportunity to freely check him out. Man, oh man, he had a sexy backside. She had always been a butt man and Jaden definitely had a fabulous ass. He was wearing a pair of loose-fitting shorts, but they didn't hide the beautiful shape. He tucked his hand in one of his back pockets and she would have given anything to be that hand. Memories of her gripping his butt, only seconds before he exploded inside her, came flooding back.

"Can I ask you a question?" Jaden said, pulling her from her thoughts.

Blinking twice, Danica realized he was standing in front of her. When did that happen? "Sure, what do you want to know?" She tried to act as though Jaden being so close didn't faze her at all when in reality her pulse raced like a stopwatch.

"I'm curious," he began, then reached down and took her hand, pulling her to her feet.

Her skin tingled on contact. "About what?"

"I'm wondering why you're not wearing an engagement ring?" he asked and dropped his gaze to her finger.

Danica snatched her hand back as if the heat of his touch burned. Oh, damn! She forgot all about wearing a ring. Standing before him, she was like a deaf-mute as she tried to think of a lie—*fast.* "I…uh…took it off. I was working at the boutique and I was afraid to get cleaner on it."

His eyes narrowed. "You haven't worn it at the garage, either."

She pursed her lips. "Too much grease and grime."

Jaden appeared amused by her answer. "In fact, I

don't remember ever seeing you wearing a ring on that finger."

Danica tilted her chin defiantly. "Maybe I just don't like wearing rings."

"Really?" His brow rose with amusement.

She swallowed the lump in her throat. "Really," she emphasized with a roll of her neck.

He stared at her for a long intense moment, then reached up and caressed her chin. "That's too bad because if you were my fiancée I'd expect you to wear my ring."

"Well, I'm not your fiancée."

His fingers traveled along her neck and cheek and she fought a shiver. "You're right. You're not." He stared down at her. "Evidently your fiancé isn't on his job, because if I bought a ring and got down on my knee and proposed, then I would want you to wear my ring for the rest of my life. I would want the entire word to know that you're the woman I planned to grow old and gray with." He continued to caress her and all she could do was stare up at him, tongue-tied. "He must have bought you a cheap ring."

Her body was starting to quiver. If she didn't do something quick she was going to find herself weakened by his touch and finishing what they had started on the desk, in his office. "It isn't cheap. I just don't wear it because I'm afraid of losing it."

"Really? I would love to see it."

"You would love to see it?"

Jaden lowered himself onto the couch. "Yeah, I would."

"Don't you have somewhere to be?" she asked, trying to buy time.

"No," he replied, then took a seat and waited.

Danica turned on her heels and headed down the

hall to her room. Goodness, now what in the word was she going to do? When she had told him she was engaged, it was only seconds before she had grabbed her bag and headed for the airport. In the last eighteen months, she hadn't heard a word from him and the only time she had seen him was at Jace's wedding, where he had totally ignored her. Never in all that time did she expect to have to produce a ring. Now what? There was no way she was going to tell him she was lying.

Once in the bedroom, Danica rummaged frantically through her jewelry box while she tried to come up with an excuse as to why she didn't have a ring. She groaned inwardly. Why didn't she just tell him it was at the jeweler's getting cleaned or that she had chipped one of the stones and was having it repaired? But she had never been good at thinking that fast on her feet.

Danica pulled out one of the drawers on her jewelry box and sighed with relief when she noticed what was inside. Nana's wedding ring. She had forgotten all about it. Along with the house and several other items of sentimental value, Nana had left the ring she had received from her second husband to her youngest granddaughter in her will. The antique setting in white gold was barely a carat and was surrounded by baguettes, but to her grandmother it had meant the world. Nana had worn it on her finger long after her husband had passed, and if she hadn't had other plans she would have worn it to her grave.

Quickly, Danica slipped it onto her finger. It was a little loose but would have to do for now. Within seconds she strolled back into the living room. "There, satisfied?" She flung her hand out. To her embarrassment, the ring flew off her finger and landed on the floor under the coffee table.

Jaden's brow rose with amusement, and Danica tried to hide her embarrassment. He was quicker than her and reached under the table and retrieved it.

"Looks like your ring is too big."

"I know that's why I haven't been wearing it. I've lost so much weight," she blurted out nervously.

He perused the length of her body. "Really?"

Damn, she was ten pounds heavier than when they had met. *Stupid. Stupid.* "My finger got smaller."

"So why haven't you gotten it sized?"

"I can't seem to part with it long enough to get it sized."

He gave her an unconvinced look. But she held her ground and with a defiant tilt of her chin, she took the ring from his hand and slipped it back onto her finger.

"It's very nice."

Gazing down at it, she nodded in agreement. "It belonged to my—oops, I mean, *his* grandmother."

"Really? Then things must be serious?"

"I already told you that."

"Really? Then why don't you have any pictures of him in here?"

"Because, because I keep them in my room."

"Really? Then go get one so I can see what he looks like."

Why is it men are always competing with each other? "I really don't feel like it."

"Well, at least tell me what he does for a living?"

"He's, uh…a lawyer."

"Really? What kind?"

"Family defense—I mean family law." She groaned inwardly. *Great thinking, Danica.*

"Where did he go to law school?"

Angrily, she waved her hands in the air. "Look, I'm tired of all these questions. Now if you'll excuse me, I need to get ready for bed."

Nodding, Jaden chuckled. "Okay, I'll let you go. I'll see you in the morning."

She followed him to the door and breathed a sigh of relief. Any more than that and he would have known she was lying. But before she could close the door, Jaden swung around.

"I hope Kenyon knows how lucky he is."

She was speechless as he reached up and stroked her cheek, then curved his hand around her neck and drew her to him. Danica barely gasped when his lips captured hers. A shiver flowed from her body to his when his tongue slipped inside her mouth. Jaden took his time and she savored everything he had to offer. He was addictive and the kisses weren't coming close to satisfying her hunger. She wanted more and to hell with the consequences. She would deal with them later. Jaden deepened the kiss and she met him stroke for stroke, knowing he wanted her as much as she wanted him. If he decided to scoop her into his arms and carry her off to bed, she would be too weak to object.

She moaned when he finally broke off the kiss, pulling them apart.

Jaden stared down at her. "That was just a little something for you to think about. I'll see you in a few hours. Sleep tight."

Danica watched him leave. Sleep was going to be hard to find.

Chapter 11

"Thanks for coming in. I hope to make a decision sometime next week."

Carrie Patrick rose from the chair and shook his hand. "Thanks, Jaden, I look forward to hearing from you." Releasing his hand, she exited his office and he returned to his seat.

The single mom was a great candidate and would be a great asset to his office. The problem was he wasn't ready yet to part with Danica. He'd already interviewed five women and he told Danica he didn't like any of the candidates. It was wrong, he knew it, but he'd lied to keep her working for him awhile longer.

"Well, what did you think of her?"

Speak of the devil. He glanced up at the door to find Danica standing in the doorway. Even in jeans and a T-shirt she took his breath away. Ever since they had watched television and shared that kiss, she had been doing everything she could to avoid him.

"She was okay."

Her brow bunched. "Okay? Okay? Jaden, Carrie's the best candidate yet."

"Maybe, but I don't think I should rush." He could tell he pinched a nerve when she propped a hand at her waist.

"Look, I've got a business to run and have spent more than enough time here."

"And have I mentioned how fabulous a job you're doing?"

"Whatever. You need to pick one of those women."

"I pick you."

She frowned, her dark brows slashing into a V. "I'm not interested in the job."

Jaden gave her a dark penetrating look. "I'm not talking about this job."

Her bottom lip quivered.

"I see you're wearing your ring today." He glanced down at the ring that had been wrapped with an excessive amount of masking tape to keep it from slipping off.

She looked pleased he had changed the subject. "I'm going to drop it by the jeweler's on my way to the boutique."

"I know an excellent jeweler." He rose. "Come on."

"Come on where?"

"We're going to walk over to Kirkland's Jeweler together. That way I can make sure they give you a good deal." Before she could object, Jaden yelled out into the garage to Kyle that he would be back in a minute, then took her hand and led her out of the building and down onto the beach.

"I don't need your help," she protested.

"I'm on lunch, so it's no bother, really."

Holding her hand, she tried to ignore the electrifying tingle as they strolled up toward the boardwalk. It was a beautiful spring morning. The ocean was calm, the sky a brilliant blue without a cloud in sight.

As they drew closer, Danica groaned inwardly. The charade was going much too far and she was getting in way over her head. She had intended to someday have her grandmother's ring sized for her pinky finger, not her ring finger. Now she was going to have to wear it and continue the story about getting engaged to Kenyon.

What a mess!

At some point, she was going to have to fake a broken engagement with her heart being shattered. That should be easy, Danica thought with a scowl. She knew firsthand how that felt.

As soon as they reached the jewelry store she paused right outside the storefront window. "Jaden, I really don't need you going in there with me."

"I told you the owner is a friend of mine. Let's go." Before she could retort, he placed a hand at the small of her back and pushed her forward into the store. The bell overhead rang, alerting a well-dressed middle-aged woman of customers. She quickly came from the back of the store and moved out onto the floor.

"Hello, Jaden. How are you doing?" she greeted, eyes wide with recognition.

"I'm doing well, Clara. Let me introduce you to Danica Dansforth." He draped an arm comfortably across her shoulders, pulling her beside him.

Clara held out a hand and greeted her. "It is definitely a pleasure."

Danica easily returned the warm smile. "The same here."

"The Beaumont family is one of my largest clients, so any friends of theirs are friends of mine. What can I do for you?"

Jaden appeared pleased by her answer. "This lovely lady needs to have her engagement ring sized."

"Engagement…" Her voice trailed off as she looked from one to the other.

Danica waited for Jaden to correct her, but instead he stood by with a silly grin on his face.

Clara appeared tickled pink and slapped her palms together. "I'll be more than happy to help you." She moved behind the counter and signaled for them to join her at the far end. "Let me see your ring."

Danica held out her hand for her to admire.

"That is a beautiful ring." She glanced over at Jaden and added, "You've got good taste."

He squeezed Danica's arm as he said, "Thank you. It belonged to my grandmother."

Danica looked over at him and blinked, wondering if she had heard him correctly. The smirk on his face was enough confirmation. As soon as Clara turned her back to them, Danica kicked Jaden in the shin. *Serves him right.*

"Ow, what did you do that for?" he whispered close to her ear.

"You know why," she managed as Clara returned with a sizer. Danica removed the ring and she slipped the bands over her finger one after the other until she found the right one.

"You're a size seven."

Clara took the ring and examined it under a glass, then looked over at Jaden and frowned. "One of your diamonds is chipped pretty badly." She showed them exactly which stone was damaged.

Danica couldn't resist giving Jaden a taste of his own medicine. "Well then, we can't have that, now, can we, darling? That is after all *your* grandmother's ring," Danica began as she stared over at Jaden while batting her eyelashes. "Clara why don't you go ahead and replace the stone and clean the others, as well?" It took everything she had not to laugh at the expression on Jaden's face. *Serves him right for making the woman think he's my fiancé.* But what he did next was not at all what she had expected.

"Sure, Clara, anything for my future bride." Jaden appeared to be more than happy to play along. He pulled Danica into the circle of his arms, and as she looked up in panic, he said, "My baby can have anything she wants as long as she continues to let me do this."

Before Danica could respond, Jaden captured her lips in a searing kiss. Closing her eyes, she lifted her hips to press against him. Her body melted and any thoughts of resisting vanished. She wasn't sure what she wanted, what she was doing, except that kissing felt right.

The kisses grew deeper and hotter and her body was completely aroused. The only thing stopping her from slipping her hands beneath his shirt was that they had an audience who cleared her throat twice, trying to draw their attention. Danica tore her mouth away to find Clara leaning across the counter smiling.

"Sorry," Danica mumbled and pushed Jaden back out of her comfort zone. He simply chuckled.

"No need to apologize. You're one lucky woman. Dozens of women in this town would kill to be in your shoes."

The look on Clara's face said she was also one of those women. Danica looked over at Jaden and frowned before turning to the salesclerk and saying, "He's not my fiancé."

"Oh, I'm sorry. I just assumed…" She looked uncomfortably from one to the other.

"Don't worry about it," Danica said with a dismissive wave. "When will my ring be ready?"

"We should have it ready by the early part of next week."

She swung her purse on her arm. "My real *fiancé* will be happy to hear that. Jaden, I'll see you tomorrow." She forced a smile, then turned on her heels and headed down the boardwalk toward the boutique.

"Don't forget my housewarming party on Saturday."
After a long evening at the boutique, Danica made it home and moved into the kitchen. Noticing the answering machine blinking, she pushed the button. As she finished listening to the message, she raised her eyebrows and swore under her breath. *There is no way I'm going to Sheyna's house without a date.*

After allowing Jaden to kiss her at the jewelry store, the last thing she needed was for him to think she was even the slightest bit interested in him. It was bad enough he had Clara thinking the two of them were engaged. Wouldn't that have been the talk of the town! Nope. She needed to find a date on her own so he'd know once and for all there was nothing going on between them.

She closed her eyes and tried to think of a solution. Calling and canceling was not even an option. Sheyna would be so disappointed and probably hunt her down and skin her alive. Danica worried her bottom lip as she gave it some thought. It wasn't as if the men were beating down her door, but then again, she had been so busy she hadn't really noticed if they were. She had been so engrossed in getting her business off the ground that her personal life had come second. She hadn't needed any distractions. Not when she had a business to open. She required all her time and energy and most men she'd dealt with in the past required a lot of time that right now she was unable to give. *Which is why you don't have a date.* Damn, she wished she had paid closer attention.

There was always Joseph.

Pulling her lower lip between her teeth, she mulled over that idea. Joseph was a nice guy. Lawyer. Recently divorced and very vulnerable. They had gone out for dinner a couple of times and each evening ended with a promise to call soon. He was a nice guy, but was transparent and too eager with his feelings. If she gave him the slightest indication that she was interested in something serious, he would jump in headfirst at the chance.

Reaching for the phone, she scrolled through her caller ID until she found his number and hit redial. The phone barely rang once before she heard his familiar voice.

"Hello, Danny."

She groaned inwardly. How many times did she have to tell him to stop calling her that? "Hello, Joseph."

"I was just sitting here thinking about calling you. How ironic is that?"

She smiled. He was so full of crap and he knew it. "What do you have planned for Saturday evening?"

"For you, I'll clear my schedule. What's going on?"

"My friend Sheyna and her husband, Jace, are having a housewarming party and I don't want to go alone."

Joseph chuckled heartily into the receiver. "Does this have anything to do with the younger brother?"

A smiled parted her lips at his comment. There was no use lying. Their platonic relationship had been straightforward from the beginning. "Yes, everything."

"No problem. I got your back."

Danica relaxed on the chair. "Thanks, Joseph."

"I'm anxious to see what my competition looks like."

She couldn't help but laugh. Jaden had used those exact words. "He's not your competition."

"Good. Maybe after this you might actually give this brother a chance."

They shared a laugh and she hung up. Her shoulders sagged with relief. Now all she had to do was find the perfect outfit.

Chapter 12

Jaden pulled his Denali onto a long driveway of a sprawling farmhouse surrounded by greenery and turned the car off. Vehicles lined both sides, which meant Jace and Sheyna had probably invited everyone who had attended their wedding plus some. He had never been big on crowds, but for his brother he would try and make an exception for tonight.

He climbed out and the scent of smoked ribs floated in the air, making his mouth water and reminding him he hadn't bothered to eat dinner.

It was almost nine. The sun had set and stars sprinkled the dark sky. Following the sounds of laughter, Jaden moved around to the back of the house and discovered the party was in full swing. Dozens of bright gold-and-green paper lanterns and torches decorated and circled the patio. Soft music was playing but was

very low under the conversations. He was pleased to see
his brother had hired a bartender.

Jaden moved over to the bar and had just ordered a
bourbon on the rocks when he spotted his brother and
his lovely wife greeting guests as they came through the
door. He shook his head. They were the perfect couple.

He loved Sheyna as if she were his own sister. After
years of knowing Sheyna and listening to her and his big
brother bickering between each other, he had always
known it was inevitable before the two of them stopped
fighting long enough to realize how much they truly loved
each other. It was definitely a big joke at their dinner table
because Jace was one man who swore there were too
many women out there for him to settle for just one.

Now look at him.

Jaden took a sip of bourbon from his glass and
glanced around the beautifully decorated room, then
studied the large group that had come to the housewarming celebration. He wished the newlyweds a long
and happy life together but that was one aisle he had no
intention of heading down. A serious relationship was
something he no longer wanted. Especially not after the
games he had played with Danica.

Hell, he hadn't thought about her in over an hour.
Ever since she had come back into his life, he couldn't
seem to get her off his mind. His mornings and nights
were filled with the one woman who had the power to
yank his heart out from his chest.

He hadn't seen her since their trip to the jewelry
store. Danica had called with some story about needing
to be at the boutique with the contractors. At the end of
the conversation she said in so many words he needed
to hurry and hire a receptionist because their time

together needed to draw to an end. What she failed to realize was that he still had her car and he wasn't ready to part with it or her just yet. Not until he got his answers and had a chance to make love to her for as many times as it took until he finally got her out of his system once and for all.

"I see you're still holding up the walls."

Jaden turned to his right and smiled wide with surprise at the tall man he spotted heading in his direction. "What's up, London? I haven't seen you in…hell, years!" He moved over and gave him a quick hug and a heavy pat on the back. The two of them went way back to high school.

London moved away and gave him a wide grin. "I heard you were back in town."

He nodded. "Yeah, almost a year now. What about you? I thought you were still in the air force?"

London shook his head. "I'm no longer on active duty. I joined a reserve unit in Dover. Family felt it was time to come home and take over my grandfather's business."

Jaden tossed his head back with a laugh. "So you're gonna be the new king of Clarence's Chicken and Fish House?"

"Yep. Actually we're expanding. I'm working on securing a second location in Wilmington."

"That's great. My boy, the entrepreneur."

"And you're still a grease monkey."

Jaden gave a shrug. "You know me. Nothing is better than holding a wrench in my hand."

London's brow rose. "I'll have to disagree. Nothing compares to holding a woman with a body like a Coke bottle."

"I see you haven't changed."

He tilted the beer in his hand and brought it to his lips. "Never." London took a sip and then someone caught his eye. "Who is that?" He gestured with his hand toward the crowd.

Jaden swung around and chuckled as a petite beauty in a short, blue spandex dress headed in his direction. "I'll give you one guess."

"Hey, you. I was wondering if you had forgotten." She came up, and Jaden slipped an arm around her waist, then dropped a kiss to her parted lips.

"Wouldn't miss it for the world." He looked over to London. "Bianca, do you remember this guy?"

She gave him a puzzled look, but it in no way matched the surprise on his face.

"Bianca? This is your little sister?" London moved beside her and took her hand in his.

"Who are you?" she asked.

Jaden did the honors. "Don't you remember London?"

Her eyes sparkled knowingly. "My, my, my, have you changed!" She gave him the once-over and Jaden didn't like the way the two of them were looking at each other.

"Bianca, don't you have somewhere else to be?"

"Big brother, relax. I'm going to go and kiss my niece. London, it was a pleasure seeing you. Hopefully, when my brother isn't looking we can maybe get to know each other a little better." She sashayed away, stopping once to glance over her shoulder and wink, then moved over to Jabarie, who was holding his daughter.

"Damn, your sister is fine!"

Jaden gave him a long look. "Yeah, and you need to stay away from her. She's too good for that."

"Yeah, yeah. Whatever. Just remember, you used to date my sister."

"Yeah, until she dumped me for an older man."

They shared a laugh, then reminisced on the old days. It wasn't long before another woman caught London's eye.

"Wow! If I had known all the women in Sheraton Beach were this fine, I would have come back home a long time ago." London nodded toward the crowd.

Jaden shifted his attention and when his gaze landed on a beautiful auburn beauty his breath whooshed out as if he'd been punched in the stomach.

Danica.

Long curls hung loosely around her shoulders. The peach dress she wore flowed along the lines of her body, accenting her narrow waist and full breasts. The color was a perfect contrast to her cinnamon complexion. No wonder a man with a receding hairline wouldn't let her hand go. Jaden's first impulse was to step forward and claim what he felt was his, to physically remove the man, but the man's wife did that for him.

For several minutes, Danica shook hands with people. From the uncomfortable look on her face they recognized her as a model. Not once did she look his way. In fact to his frustration, she carried on as if she wasn't aware of his presence. When they were dating, from the moment he had walked into a room, she'd known he was watching her. Now she seemed completely unaware of his presence and that irritated him.

But as quick as a scowl, as if she sensed his frustrations, she turned and looked in his direction. Her lips parted as if she was surprised to see him, and then just as quickly she pressed them together and looked away.

"You know her," London said, interrupting his thoughts. It was a statement, not a question. Jaden was sure the look on his face had something to do with that.

He watched her mouth, full and luscious, that demanded his attention. "Yeah…I know her," he replied without taking his eyes from her.

His penetrating gaze lingered a bit longer, then dropped to her waist, where she planted her hand as she listened to something Sheyna was saying to her. Every muscle in his lower region tightened.

How in the world could a woman have this type of effect on him after all this time? Danica laughed at something the man beside her said and placed a hand at his wrist. He was tall and lean, his cropped hair with a touch of premature gray. He wore jeans with creases that you can only get from the cleaner's and a button-down shirt. Jaden wondered if maybe there was something going on between the two of them. His blood boiled with jealousy. That should be him, *dammit!* Why did she lie about having a fiancé? Did that mean she really hadn't wanted him and the lie had just been an excuse to end things? The question was why and dammit, he was determined to find out.

Tonight.

Once again, Danica glanced across in his direction and their eyes met for a long moment and he saw something there that he couldn't read before displeasure became clear in her eyes. *Enough of the games.* Jaden threw back the remainder of his drink, then put the glass down on the table. He wanted to know who the man was standing beside her and he needed to know now.

When Danica spotted Jaden heading her way, she brought the martini glass to her lips and finished off her drink in one gulp. The closer he drew, the faster her heart pounded. She needed another drink. It would make her fourth, but there was no other way she was going to be able to get through the evening without feeling a little intoxicated, which was why she quickly sent Joseph to get her another.

Danica had come early to help Sheyna prepare for her guests. Every time she heard a car pull up her pulse raced, as she thought it might be Jaden outside. After a while she got wrapped up in the guests and relaxed her mind. And then she had known the exact moment Jaden had arrived, because whenever he was around the hairs at the nape of her neck stood to attention. Even for the last few minutes she had the feeling he was staring at her. The last several days she had been trying her damnedest to avoid him, but Danica knew coming to the housewarming party, she would run into Jaden. She wished she hadn't come. But since her new friend had been the first person to make her feel part of Sheraton Beach, there was no way she could have told her no. That was easier said than done. Of course that was before she had noticed Jaden standing over near the corner.

Before he made it halfway across the room, Jaden was detained by his parents and Danica breathed a sigh of relief. She contemplated running out the side door before he reached her, but since her car was blocked in, there wasn't too far she could go. She turned her back and pretended she was admiring a beautiful silk flower arrangement that was in the center of a large oak coffee table. It wasn't long before she felt him tap her on the shoulder. As she swung around, their eyes collided. Her gaze traveled over his rugged chocolate face.

Why did he have to be so damn sexy?

She forced a half smile. "Hey."

He grinned. "Hey. I didn't know you were coming."

"You didn't ask."

"True...I didn't." His eyes traveled the length of her. "You look beautiful."

He had always been direct. Beating around the bush was not his style. Staring up at him, she felt her heart skipping a beat. "Thank you."

Their eyes locked and after an awkward silence, he said, "This is a beautiful night."

Joseph picked that moment to return and she groaned inwardly.

"Here's your drink."

Danica forced a smile. "Thanks. Joseph, meet Jaden. Jaden, this is Joseph."

"Nice to meet you," Jaden began with his eyebrows shifted slightly. "I thought your fiancé's name was Kenyon?"

Joseph looked from him to her with a look of bewilderment. "Fiancé? I had no idea you were engaged."

Danica was sure she turned three shades red. What could she say? She definitely couldn't tell him the truth. Damn you, Jaden. He knew Joseph wasn't her fiancé! The look on Jaden's face said he was enjoying every second of this.

"Oh, yeah, she's been engaged for..." Jaden purposely allowed his voice to trail off. "Danica, it's been at least eighteen months. Isn't that right?"

The set of her mouth tightened. If she wasn't wearing three hundred dollar shoes she would have thrown one of them at his head.

"Well, Jaden, it's been really nice meeting you.

Danica, if you'll excuse me, I see someone across the room I haven't seen in years." Joseph excused himself, then quickly hurried over to the other side of the room.

Jaden stood there with a silly smirk on his face.

Tilting her chin slightly, she gave him a direct stare. "You really think you're funny, don't you?"

"What?" he began with an innocent look on his face. "I just wanted to let the brotha know he was wasting his time trying to holla at you because you're already spoken for."

Her nostrils flared slightly as she struggled to control her temper. "Jaden, I don't need you speaking for me. I can do that myself."

A hint of a smile played at the corners of his mouth. "If you say so. But it's hard for a man to know you're engaged if you're not wearing your ring."

Nervously, she placed her hand behind her back. "It should be ready on Wednesday."

"It's probably a good thing Joseph left."

She held her breath as he shifted his position until he stood in front of her, less than a foot away. "Why is that?"

He looked down at her, his expression suddenly serious. "Because I hate to have to disrespect that brotha. Dance with me."

"What?" His words caught her completely off guard. Jaden was too close. His presence was too powerful. She took a step back.

"You heard me. Let's dance." He wasn't about to let her get away. The panic banging at her heart reiterated that she wasn't as immune to him as she wanted him to think.

"There are several other women in here dying to dance with you."

"But I didn't ask them, I asked you." He gave her a

silly grin and she tried to maintain her composure while she shivered at the thought of him holding her in his arms. Dancing, liquor and Jaden were not a good combination. She glanced around looking for someone to rescue her but found no one.

"Just one song," he said, then without waiting for an answer pulled her out onto the patio.

"All right," she answered. Danica held out her hand and Jaden closed his fingers around hers and walked her out to the center of the patio floor. A shiver moved up her spine when he wound his arm around her waist and pulled her into the circle of his arms. Having him hold her this way was not a good idea and she knew it, yet she was helpless to stop it. Her body ached with need. It had been so long, too long since he'd made love to her. Yet even as she admitted she was playing with fire, she locked her arms around his neck and stared up at his intense gaze. Jaden stared back at her and she breathed in a shaky breath, capturing his scent. There was something in his entrancing gaze that was hypnotic. She felt as though she was under a spell.

Or maybe it was the alcohol.

Nevertheless, being like this in his arms slowing dancing to Baby Face reminded her of another time, another place that ended with the two of them making love on the beach. *Dammit, don't even go there.*

She tried leaning away so that their bodies didn't touch, but Jaden wasn't having it.

"Relax, I don't bite. Unless you want me to," he whispered close to her ear.

They slowly moved to the music and she was well aware how Jaden used it to his full advantage to pull her even closer. Rather than make it an issue, she tried to ignore his hard lean body pressed against hers.

"I love the way you feel in my arms."

Danica leaned back and searched his face. "Do you, really?"

"I've always loved holding you." His arms tightened around her waist. "You smell good, too."

She inhaled deeply. "Thank you." Closing her eyes, she placed her head on his chest and held him tightly, as well, and allowed the magic of the moment to take over. Jaden also smelled amazing. His cologne was subtle and sweet and perfect for him. Couples were all over the floor barely moving to the slow beat of Marvin Gaye's "Sexual Healing." Not a star in the sky. A warm gentle breeze kissed the side of her face. How she wished the caress was Jaden's lips. Leaning in closer, she was well aware he was aroused. With their bodies so close there was no way of not knowing. It was as if she and Jaden were all alone, the music playing for no one else. She couldn't remember a night since their breakup being so perfect.

As soon as he released her, she realized her heart was pounding heavily against her chest. She met his gaze that was powerful and purely sexual.

Lifting his hand, he feathered his fingers over her face in a tender caress. "Come home with me."

She wanted to run and escape because for the last several months she'd been telling herself she was over this man. But right now leaving him was the last thing on her mind. She stared at him for another long moment before she finally murmured, "Okay."

It was all the invitation Jaden needed.

"Come on." Within seconds, he had taken her hand

and was escorting her away from the party and over to his SUV. He heard Jace calling out his name. Jaden didn't bother to look his way. Instead, he tossed a hand over his head and waved. Now was not the time for small talk. He needed to be alone with Danica, *fast*.

After he helped her in on the passenger's side, he moved around to his side. Words weren't necessary as the sounds of Jill Scott filled the SUV. The ten-minute drive to his beachfront home seemed the longest of his life. Waves of yearning overcame him. He swallowed the dryness in his throat. With each breath he inhaled the subtle womanly sent that belonged to her alone. He pulled into the driveway, then opened the door and lifted Danica into his arms and carried her into the house and down the hall to his bedroom.

Once there, he lowered her onto the floor with her wrapped in his arms. To his surprise, sexual desire such as he'd never known gripped him. Anticipation doubled his pulse. He wasn't sure who started the deep passionate kisses that fed the fire burning inside him. All he knew was Danica aroused him like no other woman ever had before.

He pressed her warm body against him and cursed the clothes he still wore. Yet he hesitated to break the kiss. She tasted of alcohol and sweet apples. "Baby, I can't wait to be inside you."

"I can't wait, either," she murmured and drew his face back to her own.

Danica raised her mouth to his and the first touch sparked a fuse of fire down to his loins. Tense with control, he rewarded her with a long, slow, deep kiss. While she returned each stroke, her fingers drifted over his face, tracing the length of his jaw, threading in between his locks. He felt her body melting against him in trembling surrender.

No longer able to keep his hands to himself, he let them travel along her shoulders, across her slender back. He lowered the zipper on her dress and allowed it to fall in a pool at her feet. Jaden stepped back and sucked in a gulp of air when he looked at her naked glory.

"You're even more beautiful than I remember." Reaching out, he allowed his thumb to graze her nipple. Her sudden intake of breath nearly stole his own.

Bringing him close, Danica slid her hands underneath his shirt and trailed them up his back. He broke away and peeled off the shirt. In one swift motion, Jaden swept her into his arms and carried her over to the bed and lay down on top of her before he missed the heat of her body. Finally after weeks of trying, after months of missing her, he had the luxury of feeling the heat of her body again.

Groaning, he leaned forward and trailed his tongue along her skin, starting at her neck and shoulders. Her soft purring encouraged him to continue the exploration. Danica raised her hand and her fingertips followed the muscle play of his arms and shoulders, while he expertly kneaded and nibbled her breasts. Her breath caught and he heard her gasp from sheer pleasure.

Danica tangled her fingers in his long dark hair. The locks slid across her hand. She toyed and played with them, winding them around her fingers.

His hot breath between her breasts created a tingling inferno of pleasure. She arched up to give his mouth better access to her breasts.

"Beautiful," he murmured as he grazed one swollen

nipple between his teeth, then the other. "You taste so good." He suckled each breast in turn until the chocolate tips puckered. Then he captured a nub between his teeth and flicked his tongue over the very tip.

Jaden set the tone, yet there was no urgency in his lovemaking. He planned to take his sweet time. Damn him and his need to control! Jaden settled on top of her, pushing her thighs apart until she felt the tip of his penis pressed against her moist heat. Her own desire rose just as quickly and made her ache and grow wet. Jaden began to rock back and forth against her swollen clit. The feel of his slacks brushing her sensitive flesh only heightened her pleasure. It was also a reminder that very little stood between her and the point of no return. But Danica couldn't stop now even if she wanted to.

Bringing his mouth to her neck, Jaden told her, in searing detail, exactly what he planned to do to her.

"I'm going to make love to you, baby. Take you slowly inch by inch. And once I'm buried deep inside you, I want to feel those long legs wrapped around my waist. You want me, baby?"

Danica was speechless; mesmerized by the vision he described. She could do little but mumble in agreement.

"I didn't hear you."

"Yes," she managed to whisper.

"Yes, what?" he coaxed and reached down between them and slipped a finger inside her panties and found her moist heat. His fingers went to work and she felt air rushing in and out of her lungs.

"Please, baby!" she cried out in frustration.

"Not until you tell me what you want," he murmured, then allowed one finger to brush over her swollen bud.

Danica nearly came off the bed. "Now! I want you inside me now."

Her next breath mingled with his as he shared a deep lingering kiss. "Patience, baby. The first time's going to be hard and fast. I'll try to be gentle but forgive me, it's been a long time. But then we'll do it again…and again…and again."

She accepted every word as easy as drawing breath. He was driving her out of her mind and what his fingers were doing was pure torture. When he finally lowered her panties down over her hips, she kicked them away, her entire body trembling with anticipation. Danica was certain he was trying to steal her heart all over again, but right now it didn't matter. Nothing mattered but the man in her arms.

The air was filled with her whimpers and his soft growls. Want and need spiraled through her. Second thoughts about what she was doing were not even an issue. This was all about what Jaden made her feel. He whispered all sorts of things against her ear, and with every erotic message she could not deny the coiling tension in her body. The louder she cried out, the faster and more forcibly he ground himself against her until she convulsed in his arms. She wrapped her legs around his waist until the climax ended and he held her, raining light kisses along her face until her breathing slowed.

She wanted to come again, only this time with him fully embedded inside her. Was it a dream or was she really with the only man whom she'd ever giving her heart to?

Jaden tore his mouth from hers and kissed the skin at her throat. "I can't wait any longer. I've got to have you. I'll be right back," he whispered and climbed off her. He unfastened his belt and removed his pants, then turned and strode across the room to the door that led into his private bathroom. In the dim light of the room, Danica had a perfect view of just how aroused Jaden was. His erection created a tent inside his boxers, reminding her of the generous size of him. Danica couldn't pull her eyes away. She inhaled shakily. Her body tingled with anticipation.

As she watched him reach for a condom and slide it on, she suddenly remembered where she was and who she was with—the man who had once broken her heart. *Oh no, what am I doing?* She lifted her arms to cover her eyes and groaned. As much as she resisted, a dangerous thought flitted through her mind. Was she falling in love with Jaden again? She shook her head. That was a ridiculous thought. The alcohol made her brain fuzzy and her mind swam.

Someone called her name, and she mumbled something incoherent. There was silence and then she felt something heavy settle over her body. She snuggled into its warmth and was glad when the room stopped spinning. She managed a slurred "goodnight" before falling asleep.

Chapter 13

Danica sighed in her sleep, turned onto her side and felt something warm and hard against her hand. A man's body.

She shook off the ridiculous thought. She hadn't lain beside a man in over eighteen months. *I must still be dreaming. And when you're horny your mind has a tendency to play tricks on you.*

Satisfied with her explanation, she cuddled into the warm hard body beside her. Her head nestled in the curve of a strong shoulder. With a smile on her lips, she allowed her imagination to run wild and slid her finger-tips across a rock-hard chest, traveling lower past a patch of hair before wrapping her fingers around his—

Without warning an alarm clock went off, ruining her dream just as he rolled her onto her back. *Not yet,* she groaned inwardly. She felt as if she had just fallen asleep. When the noise refused to cease, Danica reluctantly traveled back to reality. She reached out for her clock that she always kept close on the nightstand and hit the snooze button. She wasn't ready to start her day at the boutique. Another hour wouldn't make that much of a difference. Satisfied with her decision to lie in bed just a little bit longer, Danica snuggled deeper and allowed her mind to drift off again.

"Good morning," she heard a voice say followed by a kiss to her cheek.

She knew that voice.

And those lips.

Her eyes flew open and as soon as she saw who was lying on the bed beside her, Danica shot up into a sitting position away from Jaden's warm, naked body. Amusement flashed in his eyes. *This cannot be happening to me.*

"What are you doing in my bed?" she demanded, shoving one hand through her hair while she gripped the sheets and tried to cover her breasts. Her mind was just beginning to recognize a hangover and the splitting headache that came with it.

"Actually you're in my bed. And to answer your question, I was sound asleep before you started rubbing your hands all over my body."

She shivered as his mouth curved slightly in a sleepy yet sexy smile.

Goodness, the man was sexy even in the morning. What was it about Jaden that she'd never found in anyone else? She pulled the covers higher, shielding herself from his hungry stare. *What happened last night?* Closing her eyes, she traveled back to last night and remembered dancing with Jaden under the moonlight. What happened after that was all fuzzy. She was naked and apparently so was he. Did they—

"What's running through your mind?" Jaden asked.

"Nothing," Danica mumbled. "I mean…did we…?" She purposely allowed her words to fade and waited for Jaden to understand her meaning. She watched the realization of what she was getting at.

Another smile tickled his lips. Jaden folded his hands behind his head. "You don't remember?"

"If I did I wouldn't be asking you," she snapped, then took a deep breath. No point in taking her frustrations out on him. This was just as much her fault as it was his.

He chuckled. "Relax, you fell asleep before anything important happened."

"Good." She ignored the pounding at her temples and she slipped out of bed, grabbed her panties off the floor and put them on. Jaden lay their watching her with a ridiculous grin. Her nipples began to tingle and she snatched her dress and used it as a shield before he could see the evidence of her arousal.

For heaven's sake, she'd been so drunk she had been foolish enough to come home with him. Waking up, she was all cuddled in his bed as if she belonged in his arms. He'd felt too damn good. *And he knows it.*

Jaden sat up on the bed and the sheet fell down to his hips. Danica turned her head and hoped he wouldn't get up until after she left. A woman could only take so much temptation, and seeing Jaden naked was a bit more than she could handle right about now.

That lifted brow said he knew what she was thinking. She would do anything to wipe that smirk from his face.

"What's the hurry? Now that you're awake we can finish what we started." His gaze slowly moved down her body.

Quickly, Danica stepped into the dress and pulled it up over her body. "I'm not interested in *finishing* anything, but thanks for the generous offer," she replied, and hoped to heaven her voice didn't sound as shaky as it felt.

He shifted slightly. "That's not what you were saying last night."

She gave him a dismissive wave. "I was drunk and in no way responsible for my actions. If anything I could say that you tried to take advantage of me." She swung her hair back from her face and tried to look a lot more in control than she felt at the moment. "I was drunk and what you should have done was taken me home, or better yet asked my date to take me home."

"What date? Joseph?" He paused long enough to chuckle. "The second he discovered you were engaged, he hightailed it out of there."

She propped a hand to her waist. "Yeah, thanks to you. I don't know where you…"

Her voice trailed off when he tossed back the covers in one easy motion.

Danica swallowed tightly. If he wanted to disconcert her, he knew exactly how to do it. Goodness, a woman could only take so much. A wave of something she hadn't felt in months slammed against her, taking her breath away. It took everything she had to try and act as if it didn't bother her to see him standing there in a pair of gray boxer briefs that hugged his massive thighs and tight, round—

Damn, he was sexy.

"So what you're saying," he continued as he stood and stretched lazily, "is that you had no intention of telling Joseph you were engaged until he, too, fell in love with you."

Fell in love? She searched Jaden's eyes but all she saw was an intense glare. He never truly loved her, so why was he bringing that up? Or had he? *I love you, Danica.* No, she was not about to start second-guessing her decision, although in the back of her mind she couldn't help but wonder if maybe—

Frowning, she refused to complete that thought. "I didn't tell him because there was no reason to. Joseph and I are just friends, nothing more." He was a distraction and knew it. Standing there with his massive chest and abdomen and his hard and ready— It took everything she had to drag her eyes away. "Mind your own business."

"If you say so," he said, then chuckled some more.

She stole another glance at him and found his fingers inside his boxers wrapped around the base of his—

She blew out a frustrated breath, forced herself to keep her gaze locked with his. "You're enjoying this, aren't you?"

Those sable-brown eyes glittered. "Is something wrong?" he asked and licked his lips.

Danica dropped a hand to her waist and tapped one foot against the carpet. "Yes. There is something wrong. All of this!"

Staring at her, he reminded her, "I asked you to come home with me and you agreed."

"I was drunk!" she screamed, then sighed heavily. "Can you please put on some clothes?"

"Am I making you uncomfortable?"

She rolled her eyes. The last thing in the world she was going to do was admit he made her nervous. Watching him went beyond that. He was making her feel horny as hell. "No, I make it a habit of standing and talking to naked men."

One eyebrow lifted. "We don't have to talk."

"Oh, yes, we do." She turned her back to him. There was no point in making herself crazy by trying to avoid staring at all that chocolate goodness. *Ooh*. She closed her eyes and muffled a groan at the mental image rising in her brain. "Jaden, what happened last night was a mistake."

"A mistake?" he repeated.

Swinging around, she focused on his eyes. "Yes, and it can never happen again."

"Because…"

"Because I'm engaged and what we had was over a long time ago."

Jaden dug his hands into his long hair, raising them and letting his locks slip between his fingers. "What did we have? A fling? What would you call it?"

Love. "I would call it a mistake."

Her words knocked that silly smile from his face and she almost took them back. Their time together had been special and heartbreaking and despite him breaking her heart, she wouldn't trade those few weeks for anything in the world.

"So you're saying that all the time we spent together meant nothing to you?"

"Should it? Because it definitely meant nothing to *you*."

He gave a puzzled look. "What are you talking about? Don't you remember me telling you I loved you?"

"Yeah, and the next morning I overheard you bragging about it on the phone with your brother."

"What? What in the world are you talking about?" His tone was soft and serious.

Danica dropped her eyes and turned away. "Look, it doesn't matter."

"No, we need to talk about this, because if I did something to upset you I want to know."

"That's the past and I prefer to leave it there." She struggled to put her feet in her shoes, then reached for her purse. "I'm outta here."

"Danica, wait! Let me get dressed so I can drive you home."

"Don't bother." Halfway to the door she swung around and said, "Oh, and by the way, find someone else to work at the garage, because I quit." Pivoting on her heels, she moved through the house and out the door, slamming it behind her.

Danica stormed up the road and had barely made it a block before her feet began to hurt. The high heels were definitely not made for anything other than looking pretty. Why couldn't she have walked out of Jaden's house in a pair of comfortable tennis shoes? She was tempted to go back but stubborn pride stood in her way.

The more her feet hurt, the angrier she got at Jaden. He actually thought her waking up to find herself in his bed humorous. Well, she'd showed him, and he had the nerve to pretend he had no idea why their relationship had ended.

For a moment she pondered the possibility. What if she had misunderstood that phone conversation? *Please don't let me be wrong.* As her toes began to throb, she brushed the ridiculous thought aside and moved over to the grass hoping to alleviate some of the impact. Her daddy hadn't raised no dummy. She knew what she heard—Jaden on the phone bragging about wrapping a "redhead" around his finger. *That could only be me.* For as long as she could remember people talked about her naturally reddish-brown hair she had inherited from her mother. "Red" was a nickname she'd earned way back in kindergarten.

Danica heard a car coming from behind and as bad as her feet hurt, she was tempted to stick out her thumb. *Knowing my luck, I'll get picked up by a stalker.*

The car moved alongside her and out the corner of her eye, she spotted Jaden's SUV. He was leaning out the window trying to get her attention.

"Go away!" she barked.

"Let me give you a ride," he offered.

"I don't want a ride."

"Fine, then I'll ride alongside you."

"Do whatever you want, just leave me alone!" With her head held high, she moved along the sidewalk as she tried to grit her teeth against the pain. She wasn't sure how much more she could take.

"Danica, I don't know what I said, or you think you overheard, but I never meant to hurt you."

Sure he didn't.

"Please get in, and let me drive you home. I promise I won't say a word the entire ride."

As much as she wanted to say no, her feet wouldn't let her. Pouting, Danica moved around to the passenger side and climbed in. Leaning back on the seat, she fought a groan as she pulled her shoes off.

Jaden was a man of his word and was silent the entire ride. As soon as he pulled into her driveway, she opened the door and climbed out. "Thanks for the ride," she mumbled, then swung her purse over her arm while carrying her shoes in her hand and moved up the drive in her bare feet. As soon as Jaden saw her limping, he climbed out of the car, scooped her up in his arms and carried her the rest of the way.

"Put me down," she demanded.

"Woman, please be quiet."

"Make me."

"Gladly." He pressed his mouth to her lips, silencing any further protest. She gave in to the pressure of his mouth. When he reached the porch, he took a seat on the wicker love seat and cradled her in his protective embrace as the kiss deepened. When he finally broke off the kiss, they sat there for the longest time staring at each other, neither of them speaking until a voice coming from next door drew their attention.

"Good morning."

At the sound of the high-pitched voice, they both looked over to find Mrs. Graves on her porch watering her geraniums.

"Good morning," Danica replied with an inward groan. The last thing she needed was for her nosy neighbor to think there was something going on between the two of them, yet when she tried to move from Jaden's lap, he refused to let her leave, keeping his hand planted firmly at her waist.

"Good morning, Mrs. Graves," Jaden replied.

Mrs. Graves gave them a dismissive wave and a warm smile. "Don't you lovebirds mind me at all. There's nothing better than seeing young people in love."

"We're not..." Danica's words trailed off as she watched her neighbor walk back into the house. *Great. Just Great.* She pierced Jaden with a heated stare. "Look what you did! You got that old woman thinking we're an item."

"We would be if you'd stop playing games."

"Who's playing games?"

"We're both attracted to each other."

"Speak for yourself."

"Quit denying it. You're still just as attracted to me as you were when we first met. Hell, I'm not ashamed to admit it."

She paused. "Okay, so maybe I am a little attracted to you, but so what? Things can never go back to the way they were."

"Why?" he asked, looking a little confused.

"Because I'm engaged."

"This isn't about him. This is about you and me," he said quietly.

"There's no you and me."

Jaden kissed her. "I think there is." Danica got ready to say something, and he leaned in and silenced her with another kiss. "Now are you ready to listen?"

Nodding, she caught her lip between her teeth.

"I have a proposal for you."

She swallowed. "What kind of proposal?"

"I propose a sexual relationship. No commitments. No heartache. Just pleasure."

"What?"

Jaden's eyes glittered as he looked at her. "It would give us both a chance to get each other out of our system while receiving a little sexual satisfaction at the same time."

Danica grunted. "Why in the world would I agree to that?"

"Because you're about to marry another man yet you're still attracted to me. I think you at least need to be sure of your feelings before you marry him. You owe your fiancé at least that."

Oh, brother. This whole fiancé thing was starting to get on her nerves.

"Do you have any idea how much I want you, Danica?"

She stared up into his eyes and saw hunger. The reason she recognized it was that she was feeling it, as well. Briefly, she closed her eyes before she said softly, "Yes, I think I do."

"I want you to know that if you agree, I intend to focus all my energy on you. The second I leave the garage at night, I plan to spend every evening making love until we're both satisfied and exhausted. Do you know how badly I want to kiss you starting at your feet and work my way slowly up to your lips, tasting everything in my path?"

A lump formed in her throat and she tried to swallow. She so desperately needed to breathe. His proposal sounded so tempting, but could she really just walk away when it was over with her heart still intact?

She opened her mouth to say something, but Jaden placed a finger to her lips, silencing her. "Shhh, not yet. I know I've given you a lot to think about. Take a couple of days to consider my offer."

He rose and lowered her slowly to her feet, holding her still and close. With her body resting against his, she was aware of her nipples brushing against his solid chest.

"Here's a taste of what I have to offer."

And taste was exactly what she received. Jaden dipped his head down and claimed her lips. An ache stirred in her chest, then traveled lower to her stomach. His tongue found hers, and Danica groaned in response. Hungry for his touch, she arched toward him, her nipples grazing against his chest. He gathered her closer, his hands going to her bottom, lifting her firmly against him, their clothing a barrier that added friction to their passion. His kiss, his touch was doing crazy things, making her think about things that weren't even possible.

He groaned as her palms caressed his back, and then just when she thought he'd carry her into the house, Jaden pulled back, his tone serious, and said, "I look forward to your answer."

Danica wasn't sure how long after he left that she was still standing there before she finally went inside the house.

Chapter 14

Jaden raised a dark brow. "What do you mean Danica left town?"

Sheyna placed her glass of lemonade back on the table. "Just what I said. She left town."

There had to be some kind of mistake. "How do you know?"

"Because I'm the one who drove her to the airport," she said with ridicule.

Lips pressed firmly together, Jaden moved over to the sliding glass and stared out at his brother trying for the third time to light the barbecue grill. He would go out and offer his assistance, but right now he had other things on his mind. Mainly, Danica. How in the world did she leave town for the weekend without telling him?

Not that she had to answer to him. She was free to see whomever and do whatever she wanted, but he had hoped that after his proposal she would have taken a day or two to consider it. Instead an entire week had passed without a word, and now Sheyna had the nerve to tell him she had left town.

He swung around and returned his full attention to her. "Where did she go?"

"Maybe to see her fiancé," Sheyna said with an amused look.

Jaden scowled, letting her know he didn't see anything funny at all, and she sobered slightly.

"I don't know exactly. Danica said something about doing a benefit fashion show."

Her words eased his mind a bit, yet it still bothered him to know that she left town without saying a word. Did he really mean that little to her?

He didn't even know why it even mattered especially when all he was interested in was getting her out of his system once and for all. But even as he finished that thought he knew that that was no longer the case. Things had changed. His feelings had changed and as much as he tried to fight it, he knew Danica meant so much more to him than that. He wanted her to be a part of his life. The question burning in his mind was, how did Danica feel about him?

On Monday, Danica strolled into the nightclub just in time for happy hour. She definitely needed a drink.

The last three days had been long and hard and reminded her why she had been so eager to leave modeling behind. This morning she had gotten a good night's sleep and caught an afternoon flight into Philadelphia. On her way down to the beach, she had retrieved her messages and when she got one from Sheyna asking her to join her for happy hour at Niko's, she jumped at the chance. Danica stopped at home long enough to roll her suitcase into the house and change into a short blue-jean skirt and a lemon-colored halter top with matching espadrilles.

Moving across the floor, she couldn't help swaying her hips to the beat of Alicia Key's hit single, "Not the One." *How appropriate.*

That was exactly what she had been thinking when she had left town without letting Jaden know she was leaving or her whereabouts for the last couple of days. But the last three days she'd had plenty of time to think and realized she was only fooling herself. Danica had missed him like crazy.

I never stopped loving him.

She had no idea being away from Jaden would have that kind of affect on her. Now all she could think about was being with the man she loved. She wanted him with everything she had even though she knew there was no way she could protect her heart from being hurt again. Once she agreed to his proposal, there was no turning back. Was she really ready to risk her heart again? That was a question she wasn't sure she knew how to answer until she saw him again. However, her plan was to join Sheyna, then drive over to Jaden's and talk to him. That kind of bravado was going to require a drink…or two.

After glancing around the room, Danica spotted Sheyna sitting in a booth to the far right. She strolled over and joined the group.

"There you are!" Sheyna exclaimed and slid over so she could sit beside her. "I was hoping you were coming. You know my sisters-in-law, right?"

"Sure, I met them at your wedding." Danica's smiled

as she greeted the two women. There was Brenna Gathers-Beaumont, who was married to Jabarie, and his lovely sister, Bianca.

Brenna reached her arm across the table and shook her hand. "Of course I remember meeting you. I didn't get a chance to talk to you then, but I wanted to say that you're even prettier in person."

Danica loved the way Brenna's eyes crinkled when she smiled. "Thank you."

Bianca was brimming with excitement. "I wanted to model once, and followed your career for years."

"Quit before you make me blush." Even after ten years, Danica was always amazed at how anyone cared enough to want to follow in her footsteps.

As she cupped her chin in her palm, Bianca's smile deepened. "I'm serious. Everybody is talking about your boutique."

Her eyes widened with excitement. "Really?"

"Oh, yeah," Brenna confirmed. "Word gets around quickly around here. A fashion model living in our town, I guarantee the newspaper is going to do a front-page story."

Danica gave her a nervous smile. "Actually, they contacted me last week about doing an interview."

Bianca clapped her hands. "See! I told you. Before you know it your boutique is going to be flooded with customers."

"I sure hope so. It's been a long hard road and I'm cutting it so close I was starting to worry."

Sheyna gave her a dismissive wave. "You don't have anything to worry about."

Bianca agreed. "If you need some help, I'll be more than glad to come over and help you."

"Me, too," Brenna replied. "I could use a break from Arianna and Jabarie. Don't get me wrong. I love being a mother but sometimes I need a little *me* time."

Danica nodded in agreement. Even though she didn't have any kids, she knew what it was like to rarely have any free time.

The waitress arrived and took all their drink orders. Danica and Bianca ordered cosmopolitans and Brenna a margarita. Sheyna asked for a soda.

"Since when do you order a Sprite at happy hour?" Brenna asked with curious scrutiny as soon as the waitress left.

Sheyna's eyes traveled around the table, and then she smiled as she said, "Since I found out I'm pregnant."

"What?"

"Oh, my goodness!"

The three started screaming and congratulating her at the same time.

"When did you find out?" Bianca asked, breathless.

"Three days ago."

"Three days? I'm supposed to be your best friend. How could you keep it from me that long?" Brenna asked, trying to hide her grin behind a frown.

"Believe me, I wanted to tell you so bad but I wanted to wait until Jace got back from visiting the Beaumont Hotel in Virginia Beach."

Danica leaned across the table. "What did he say when he found out?"

Her eyes sparkled as she spoke. "When he got home I had baby books scattered all over the bedroom, kitchen and living room. It wasn't until Jace sat down to eat that he noticed the book Eating for Two. He dropped his fork and looked over at me. All I could do was nod."

The ladies laughed.

Bianca nudged her sister-in-law in the shoulder. "Brenna, you own the Cornerstone Bookstore. How could you not know what was going on when she came in and bought all those books?"

She shrugged and smiled. "I guess I must have been on break or something."

Sheyna gave her a sly look. "Exactly. I knew if you knew what I was buying there would be no way you could keep it from your husband."

Brenna pretended to look offended. "I know how to keep a secret."

"Yeah, right," she teased.

Bianca clapped her hands together with animated excitement. "I'm so happy for you! I'm going to be an auntie again."

Brenna gave a rude snort. "It's about time. Our children are supposed to grow up together."

"They will now," Sheyna replied with a huge grin on her face.

They sat around talking about baby names until the waitress arrived with their drinks.

"I hope that's water in that glass."

At the deep baritone voice, the women looked to see Jace moving up to the table.

Sheyna grinned. "Soda, baby. I promise I'm not trying to make your baby an alcoholic." She tilted her head in time for him to press his lips to hers.

"Congratulations, big brother," Bianca said, and the others joined in.

"Thanks," he replied, beaming with pride.

Danica was listening to Brenna teasing her brother-in-law with stories of the delivery when the hairs at her nape stood on end. She glanced across the floor and spotted Jaden sitting at a table with Jabarie, staring directly at her. Her pulse ricocheted. She had no idea the Beaumont brothers were going to be here. If she had, she wouldn't have come. Yet now that she was here there was no way she could even have thought about running away. She couldn't move even if she had wanted to.

Damn, I love that man.

The music changed to Heather Headley's "In My Mind." Other than her sweet melody, it was as if the rest of the world no longer existed.

Jaden rose from the chair and slowly moved toward her with his eyes never leaving hers. With every step her heartbeat raced. She tried taking a deep breath and calming herself, but it was useless.

Why did he have to be so fine? she thought as he slowly closed the distance that separated them. He was wearing a pale green button-down shirt and a pair of black Dockers. The color looked remarkable against his skin. But it was more than what was on the outside that attracted her to him. Jaden continued to hold her gaze, and stirred something inside her that no other could. He made her feel things she just couldn't begin to put into words.

As he drew nearer, warning bells went off in her head, telling her to put her defensive wall back up, but it was too late. Jaden reached out and offered her his hand.

And she accepted.

Together they moved out onto the dance floor. He wrapped his arms around her and with a will of their own, her arms moved around his neck, where she locked her hands. As they moved to the beat of the music, Jaden's intense gazed beamed down at her.

"Hello, Danica."

"Hello."

"How was your trip?"

She smiled. He knew she had left town. "Long, but it benefited a good cause."

"Glad to hear that." Their eyes locked. "I missed you."

"Oh, really?" she began with a hint of cockiness. "What did you miss?"

"Talking to you. Smelling you." He leaned in closer long enough to press his lips to her cheek. "Have you thought about my proposal?"

"Somewhat."

"I guess that means you haven't made a decision about letting me make love to you."

Make love to you. Damn, she hadn't been this aroused since the first time she realized she loved him.

And she still did. God help her, she did. But too much time had passed. She was older. Wiser and smart enough to know there was no way to go back.

"What makes you think I'm interested?" she finally said.

"If you weren't you would have told me off by now. Your voice wouldn't have softened and your—"

"My voice hasn't softened," she protested, although she knew it had.

A smile teased the corner of his mouth. "Whatever you say." He kissed her cheek again. "Will you stay with me tonight?"

The thought of spending another night with him made her feel nothing short of tingly. This was what she had dreamed about.

"What's it going to take to convince you?"

"Convince me of what?"

"That I am still attracted to you. There is still something brewing between us and before you can move on and marry another man, you need to finish what we started."

After a long moment, she slowly nodded as she said, "You're right. No point in going into a new relationship if I still got the hots for another man."

"So you admit that you do still have the hots for me?"

"I…" She couldn't help but smile at his irresistible grin. "Yeah, I'll admit that I am attracted to you but it's physical, nothing more," she lied.

"Then that makes two of us."

She reached for her glass and took a sip.

"So does that mean we have a—"

"Hush." She leaned forward and placed a finger to his lips. A smile curled his lush lips. Their faces were mere inches apart. She dropped her voice to a seductive whisper. "Anybody ever tell you you talk too much?"

His tongue slipped out and licked the tip of her index finger. A delicious heat traveled down her arm to her breasts, causing her nipples to harden. The brief touch made her want to reach out and touch him.

Jaden stopped dancing. "Come on, let's go."

Her heart raced with anticipation. "Where are we going?"

"How about dinner first, then we can talk about dessert?"

He stared at her eyes, assessing her. This was her last chance to reconsider her decision to engage in a sexual relationship. All she had to do was find him a receptionist while he fixed her car, and for an added bonus she got no-strings-attached sex. Then they could both go their own separate ways and she could finally forget about him.

She moved off the dance floor and he took her hand and had started to lead the way when he paused and turned around. His mouth closed over hers and she welcomed the sweet warmth of his lips, enjoying the pressure of his body against her.

He broke off the kiss and buried his face in her hair. "I've been wanting to do that all week."

She too had been waiting for him to kiss her again. But unlike him she wanted something special, something more than a few hours or sex. She wanted to be held, touched, caressed. She wanted to be loved but she wasn't foolish enough to believe that was something Jaden could offer her. Instead she would continue to play the game, the bride-to-be getting her ex-lover out of her system once and for all. There was no way she would ever let him know she still loved him.

Placing a hand on the small of her back, he led her out of the bar and to her car.

Before opening the door, she stopped and turned to him. "I don't think what happened between us is something that's going to easily go away. But I want you to know one thing." Her heart pounded wildly inside her. "I'm crazy about you," she said candidly. "And for that I accept your proposal."

He sighed and moved closer. "I hope you're ready for the ride of your life. Because I plan to have my fill of you."

His words stirred a yearning in her chest, but Danica refused to lead her heart into such danger again. But she wanted this moment with him, wanted a chance to rediscover what they'd had together, and get him out of her system once and for all.

"I like the way that sounds," she whispered huskily, and then he covered her mouth.

Danica sank into his kiss. The feelings she'd kept locked inside were threatening to break loose. The last thing she wanted was for Jaden to know how she felt. Could she hide her feelings? Despite the vow she made to herself, she wanted to be with him again. Could she indulge in an affair with him and leave with her heart intact?

Knowing that she still loved him, she didn't think she could. But she loved him and for that reason and that reason alone she wanted this time with him no matter how short and no matter how painful it might be in the end. Hopefully, she too would be able to work him out of her system. Yep, she was ready to face the consequences of being lovers again.

Jaden opened a bottle of champagne, his thoughts still on Danica. He poured them both a glass and waited for her to come out of the bathroom. They had had dinner at Murray's Steakhouse. The entire time his body had hummed with anticipation for the evening to come. By the time the waiter brought the check, they were both stroking each other underneath the table. Laughing, they raced out to their vehicles and after another searing kiss, they hurried back to his place.

Hearing movement behind him, Jaden turned to watch Danica come out of the bathroom in nothing but sexy underclothes. Scraps of black lace barely covered her full breasts and thatch of curls. Her sweet cashew skin looked soft and delicate. Long legs, high, firm breasts and a flat belly.

"Damn!" was all he could muster to say.

She strolled over to where he was standing and took the flute from his hand and took a sip. "Mmm, that's good," she purred, then sashayed over to the window and looked out at the ocean.

Jaden watched the sway of her hips, then moved behind her and wrapped his arm around her middle. She offered him a sip of her champagne and while staring out at the raging tide, they finished her glass.

His mouth brushed her neck. At the feel of his lips against her skin she sighed. Jaden took the flute from her hand and tossed the empty glass over onto a nearby chair. He would get it later. Right now he had more important things to attend to.

He swung her around to face him. Their gazes locked and held as she arched against him, her expression daring and seductive. He leaned forward and pressed his lips to hers while reaching behind her and releasing her bra and allowing it to fall to the floor.

"Turn around."

She obeyed and he moved behind her. Grasping her breasts from behind, he watched her face in the glass as he fondled them. As her nipples peaked beneath his fingertips, her lips parted. When he shifted her legs apart, he looked down at the lace thong between her buttocks and grinned. His fingers slid across her skin and down the crease of her thigh, between her legs. He was amazed at how wet she already was. Clutching the rim of her thong he ripped it from her body.

Blood pounded in his veins. He continued to stroke her. Her breathing labored like his own. Jaden reached up and stroked her inner thigh and moved higher.

Oh, me.

Oh, my.

Why was she getting turned on again so soon? Her body yearned for something long and thick that only Jaden could give her.

As if he could read her mind, he touched her clit. Danica sucked in a gasp, then squirmed. He urged her to lean against the sliding door. She cried out when her nipples touched the cold glass.

"Jaden," she moaned.

"I'm right here, baby."

She was in turmoil. Her nipples and belly constricted from the cool glass, but the heat of his body was enough to keep her warm.

"This glass is cold," she whispered.

"I'm about to warm you up."

Instead of backing away, he squeezed his hands between her body and the glass. His rough palms covered her breasts, and the resulting heat shocked her. He took a hardened nipple and rolled it between his fingers. Danica moaned with delight. He created such a fervor she could hardly stand it. "Oh, that feels good."

She shuddered, and then he removed one hand and reached between them and unbuckled his pants, and she heard them drop to the floor. She could feel the length of his penis throbbing between her parted thighs. Her body trembled with anticipation.

"Do you know how hard it was not seeing you this week? Do you know how badly I've been wanting to be inside you?" He pressed his full lips to the back of her neck and desire shot through her veins.

"Yes," she whispered.

"Damn, I wanted you. I was just afraid to start something between us again," he said huskily.

"And now?"

"There's something about you I can't resist. That makes me want to take that risk." He pinned her with the weight of his body. She quivered and sucked in a breath as his hands roamed freely. To her breasts. Across her hips. Along her thighs. He slid his fingers along her stomach and smoothed downward until they tangled in her curls.

"Oh!" she whimpered. She was eager to have him. His fingers swirled and played in her damp cropped hair.

He slid one foot between hers and nudged her legs apart, spreading her thighs to give him better access. Her muscles quivered as she waited for him. Finally, his hand covered her mound. She shuddered on contact. His fingers slid along the doors of heaven, making her legs tremble. She groaned. She was out of her mind with lust. He finally rubbed against her clit and the friction made her jump. Jaden pushed against her several times, and she whimpered and rocked and felt cream running down her inner thighs.

Danica rolled her forehead against the glass door. Her hot air had fogged the top half of the glass. Anybody looking in from the outside would have a view of her naked body. The thought only heightened her arousal.

"Are you ready for me?" he whispered.

Ready? She was about to come unglued. He eased between her folds and pushed two fingers up into her.

"Ahh!" she cried out. Oh, was it good!

"Damn, you're tight."

The strain in his voice nearly matched hers. His fingers plunged deep, hard and fast. Little sounds left her throat. Her hips rocked against him and soon more evidence of her arousal ran down her thighs.

Tremors started radiating from her belly. Immediately, he moved her legs even farther apart. She spread her palms wide on the smooth surface of the glass and braced herself. He released her long enough to reach down for his pants and removed a condom from his pocket. As soon as the condom was on, Jaden bent his knees and positioned himself. She had barely taken a breath before he surged straight up inside her. She cried out sharply at the contact. Jaden swore under his breath and pulled back.

"Did I hurt you?" he asked, voice laced thickly with concern.

"No." She hadn't had sex in nineteen months. "Please, I need you inside." She wiggled her butt against the length of him and to her relief, he pushed upward again. This time her body stretched to make room for him. Within seconds, he found a rhythm and was soon pounding into her with long, deep thrusts.

Danica felt herself losing control. Pain had turned into pleasure. Oh, she needed this. She'd needed him. "Jaden!" she cried. An orgasm was so close she could taste it.

He began stroking. Out. In. Out again. Each hard thrust lifted her right up on her tiptoes. Tremors took over her body, and she let out a scream as the orgasm hit with mind-boggling intensity. He rode her hard until she collapsed against the glass.

Abruptly, he pulled out of her. Danica whimpered at the sudden loss. Jaden turned her around. Their eyes met, and she saw a playful gleam when he lifted her into his arms.

"Wrap your legs around my waist," he ordered between ragged breaths. She obeyed and before she had a chance to prepare, he plunged back inside her. "How's that feel?" he groaned between pumps.

"Uh-huh," she moaned. "Good. Damn good."

She leaned forward, and he took advantage of the access to her breasts. Coming forward, he closed his mouth over one dark nipple and sucked. Danica arched away from the glass, pressing firmly against his mouth. She tightened her legs around his waist and rocked her hips back and forth, rubbing her clit against his penis. Inside her, she could feel him pulse and knew he was about to lose it. He leaned back, leaving her breasts, wet and aching.

"Get ready, baby. I'm getting ready to come," he hissed, lips against her ear.

With both hands, he gripped her behind and plunged hard. It didn't take long before he came inside her. Eyes locked, she watched the reaction on his face as he groaned between clenched teeth. It made her feel good to know she brought him such satisfaction.

Completely spent, Jaden sagged against the door with her securely in his arms. Her body trembled; her brain was a complete blank. She felt his finger glide across her clit and that was all she needed. She cried out as her body convulsed and she came one last time.

"Thank you," she whispered moments later.

"For what?" he asked between heavy breaths.

Feeling slightly uncomfortable, Danica lowered her eyelids. "For reminding me what it was like."

Breathing harshly, Jaden planted a kiss on her mouth. "It's only the beginning." Leaning forward, he blew against her nipple and Danica shivered.

How could it possibly get any better than this? "What else do you have in store for me?" she asked.

"You'll have to wait and see."

"I can't wait." Danica was still holding on as he carried her to the shower.

Chapter 15

The next week Jaden constantly surprised Danica with intimate dinners, a cruise on his yacht under the moonlight, a movie with a huge bucket of popcorn and a salsa dance lesson. Charming, funny and handsome, Jaden made each and every moment special and memorable. Danica sighed with contentment every evening when he held her in his arms after making love to her. Their physical relationship was something that she couldn't seem to get enough of. The more they came together the more she wanted.

With all the time they spent together, nothing could have amazed Danica more than when Jaden asked her to dress comfortably and ride with him on Wednesday to Dover.

He picked her up from the boutique at six and drove thirty minutes into an area of town she had never been to before and pulled up in front of the Dover Boys & Girls Club.

"What are we doing here?" she asked while opening the passenger side door.

"I volunteer my time here a couple of hours a month."

Her brow rose. She was clearly impressed. "I used to mentor young girls with self-esteem issues."

He looked equally impressed. "We could use more volunteers. Anything to help keep the kids off the street."

Taking her hand, he led her inside and onto a basketball court where at least two dozen teenagers were hanging out.

Some were in shorts, T-shirts and expensive gym shoes, playing competitive basketball. A small group was cheering from the sidelines. Another group at the far end of the court was playing rap music from a boom box and doing a popular new dance that she'd recently seen on BET and enjoyed watching, but couldn't begin to imitate. A few girls sat on the stands, leaning back on the bench, popping chewing gum and talking on cell phones. When the players spotted Jaden and Danica coming across the court, the game stopped and all eyes were on them.

"Whassup, J?" a kid holding a ball under his arm said with a jerk of his chin.

"Whassup with you, Tyrese? How you do on that driving test?"

He grinned with pride. "I aced it."

"Congratulations." He moved over and gave him dap and spoke to the rest of the team.

"Who's this?" Tyrese asked, eyeing her with interest.

"This is my friend, Danica Dansforth."

His eyes perused her length. "Man, you tall! You some kinda model or something?"

"She used to be."

Tyrese looked from Jaden to Danica with intrigue. "Really? You ever pose for that magazine that always have them women in swimsuits?"

She held up her fingers. "Twice."

The boys all started howling, and one yelled over to the bleachers, "We got a celebrity in the house!"

One of the girls from the bleachers called out, "Whatever! We're here to watch a game."

"Can you play?" Tyrese asked, catching the ball on a return throw.

"There's only one way to find out." She released Jaden's hand. "Get me the ball."

Tyrese tossed it to Danica. She caught it and began to dribble the ball. "I'll have you know, I was all-American for two years," she said, maneuvering around a player who tried to block her. Picking up speed, she jumped into the air and shot the ball into the basket.

The girls on the bleachers started cheering.

"Damn! Beauty and skills. J, you one lucky dude," Tyrese said, giving him dap.

She and Jaden then joined in a competitive game that ended with her making the final shot and winning the game. Afterward, the girls moved over from the bleachers to congratulate her.

"You think maybe you could teach me how to model?" asked a slender girl with curly hair. The girl to her right pushed her in the shoulder and gave her a look that said she couldn't believe she asked such a question.

Danica nodded. "I would love to. I'll talk to the program director about scheduling something."

The girls looked pleased by her answer.

Jaden and Danica waved to the group, then headed back out to his truck. He took her hand and pulled her close to him, then draped his arm across her shoulders. Even though she was sweaty and probably smelled bad, she marveled at the sensation she felt from his touch and snuggled against his chest.

"I didn't know you could play basketball," Jaden said and kissed the top of her head.

"My father brought my brother and me up on the basketball court. He played in high school, even received a full scholarship to college. Unfortunately he blew out his knee his sophomore year. He made it clear that if we wanted to go to college, we had to find a way to pay for it. My brother and I were natural born athletes. He got a scholarship to Purdue and I played basketball all through high school until I started modeling."

"You're full of surprises."

"So are you. Thanks for bringing me tonight. It was fun."

"It's nice to get out of the garage from time to time. I've even invited the boys down to help me change oil on occasions."

"That's nice of you."

"Anything to keep them off the streets. Most of them don't have fathers at home. Tyrese's two older brothers are both serving time in the penitentiary. His mother is trying to do everything she can to keep him from following in their footsteps. So far she's doing a good job. He works part-time stocking shelves at the grocery store and finally earned enough money to buy himself a car."

"That's good to hear."

They reached his truck and he pushed a button on his keychain and turned off the alarm. She waited until he had started the car and pulled away from the parking lot before she asked, "What made you decide to volunteer?"

He shrugged. "Somebody has to. My family's been doing it for years. Of course, now that Jace and Jabarie have families they don't spend as much time mentoring as they used to. Bianca volunteers at the elementary school's reading program. Sheyna does an auction every year to earn money."

Danica nodded. She was supposed to have been one of the bachelorettes participating in an auction almost two years ago. But she had suddenly gotten ill with a stomach virus. A smile curled her lips at the memory of Jaden coming over and taking care of her all weekend. That was when she had first realized she had fallen in love with him.

As she glanced over at Jaden's profile, a warm feeling flowed through her chest. With a sigh, she leaned her head on his shoulder, and knew without a doubt that she still loved him. Letting go a second time was not going to be easy.

Moving over to his SUV, Jaden glanced over his shoulder at Danica's house, hoping to catch a glimpse of her through the window. Just moments ago, after he rose from her bed and kissed her lips, she had asked him to lock the door behind him and was probably now sound asleep.

Jaden unlocked the car and looked over at the house once more. He blew out a deep breath as he climbed in and realized he had it bad. No matter how many times he made love to her, he couldn't remove her from his system. All the loving would do was make him want her more, until he possessed all of her.

Raking a frustrated hand across his locks, he growled. He had offered her a proposal to get out of each other's system. It was supposed to be just sex, so why were the feelings between them so strong and intense?

He leaned back on the seat and glanced up at her room and wished he had stayed.

Ending the relationship was the last thing he wanted. He'd spent the last several months ignoring his emotions, but he couldn't any longer. At one point, it seemed more important to react and feel everything he could with Danica until the wick ran out. A few stolen moments were better than none at all. But now his body already craved more. And he had this strong determination to have her again and again until he made her his completely. Inside his brain was a war. Half his brain wanted to see where the relationship went. Hell, he imagined waking up to her every morning for the rest of his life. The other half of him wanted to run far away. He'd been running for the last several months, and for the first time he had someone who made him want to stop. Only, he had already been here once before with Danica and this time he was too afraid to admit what he was feeling quite yet. But he knew he would have to eventually. It just seemed that time was going to come more sooner than later.

Chapter 16

Danica spent the afternoon cleaning her house. After vacuuming the living room, she moved up to her bedroom. Pulling back the bedspread, she stripped the sheets from her bed and brought them to her nose.

Jaden.

Closing her eyes, she allowed herself time to indulge in the masculine scent that was all his own. Visions of the night before with the two of them riding to a feverous climax danced before her eyes.

After leaving the Dover Boy & Girls Club, they had returned to her house and shared a shower. Once he pressed his lips to her back they made love long after the water ran cold. She then made a simple dinner of salads with grilled chicken and after sharing a glass of wine curled up on the couch, the two raced up to her bedroom, where Jaden made love to her again until well past midnight.

Even now her body responded to the way he made it feel as his lips traveled from her toes to her lips, stopping at several places along the way. Another shiver passed through her and she quickly opened her eyes and finished stripping the linen.

Danica moved to the linen closet and removed a clean set of sateen sheets and returned to her room. While she made her bed, she tried to figure out what she was going to do now that she had discovered she was in love. By the time the bedspread was neatly in place, she accepted the truth. She'd never stopped loving him.

All last year she had tried to bury her pain behind her work by pouring all her energy into opening her boutique, but now that he was back in her life, she could no longer deny the obvious. What in the world was she going to do when it was time to walk away?

After spending another hour cleaning house while trying to sort out her feelings, Danica screamed, "Enough!" then mentally shifted gears and spent the rest of the day at the boutique.

It was starting to come along nicely. The dressing rooms were ready. The shelves had all been hung and the merchandise lining the walls in boxes, was ready to be hung on racks that were to be assembled tomorrow. At this rate she would be ready to open in another week. A smile curled her lips. It was a long haul but hard work had finally paid off.

After an hour, she finally decided to take a break and moved into her office to remove a bottle of water from the small portable refrigerator. The phone rang, and she moved over to her desk and picked it up. "Hello?"

"Hey, baby. How's your day?"

Danica smiled at the sound of Jaden's deep velvety voice. "Better now that I'm talking to you."

"How about I make dinner for you tonight?"

She bubbled with excitement. "That sounds like a plan."

"Good, I'll see you at seven."

"I'll be there," she said in parting. After hanging up, Danica glanced over at the clock. She had three hours. That gave her just enough time to finish her inventory, then go home and get ready.

As she climbed out of the car and made her way across the yard, her stomach churned with anxiety. Would he be able to tell she yearned for a future with him? Oh, God, she groaned, I hope not. After she pressed the doorbell, it wasn't long before she heard footsteps and the door swung open.

"Perfect timing." Jaden greeted her with a smile.

Her gaze took in everything as he loomed in front of her in a brown shirt and chocolate shorts that showed off athletic legs and calves. On his feet were a pair of leather sandals.

He stepped aside so she could enter, and she realized her hands were shaking. She had been impatiently waiting all day to see him again.

"I brought dessert," Danica said breathlessly.

Jaden smiled. "I'm not gonna lie and say I didn't want you to bring anything, because I'm glad you did." The caressing sound of his voice was music to her ears.

Jaden took the pie from her hands, and she glanced around as she stepped into the living room. Oak floors, cream walls and antique furniture with blue as a complementary color created a light and masculine atmo-

sphere. A formal dining room was to her right, a staircase straight ahead. She chuckled inwardly. All the
times she had been at his house, they'd had other things
on their mind, and it had been too late to admire his
home. "You have a nice place."

"Thanks. Since I moved in I haven't had much time
to make but a few changes."

One thing she liked was the floor-to-ceiling
vertical blinds that allowed sunlight to flood both
rooms. She moved to the mantel and picked up one
of the small elephants.

"Ooh, pretty! You a collector?"

"Yes. I've been collecting them for about two years
now." He stood behind her, his warm breath on her
neck. She didn't dare move. The warmth of his body
felt so comforting she wanted the feeling to last as long
as possible.

"They're beautiful," she whispered.

"So are you."

Danica slowly turned to face him. Those three words
still vibrated through her. Her heart sped up and her
breathing became shallow as she stared up at him.

"I missed you today."

She swallowed at the admission. "So did I."

Jaden tilted his head slightly and stared intensely at
her, his expression was serious. "You've managed again
to work your way into my head."

Her eyes widened in amazement. That was the last
thing she had expected to hear, but she felt the same
way. Now if only she could manage to work her way
into his heart.

She couldn't get him off her mind. Being with him,
she was dying to feel his arms, his lips. As if he read

her mind, Jaden leaned in and pressed his mouth to hers. His tongue sent desire blazing through her body.

Danica responded by wrapping her arms around him. There was no mistaking his erection that was pressed against her stomach. She pulled him close yet it still wasn't close enough. "We better stop or we'll be eating dinner later," she said.

With a sigh, he released her, and she noticed his eyes shimmered with enough passion to steal her heart. Taking her hand, Jaden led her into the kitchen to a small screened-in deck out back with a breathtaking view of the ocean.

For the next couple of hours, he was the perfect host. He had grilled steaks, baked potatoes and a garden salad and iced tea. Afterward, they played a competitive game of Scrabble. Nightfall had descended on Sheraton Breach like a translucent veil when they stepped out onto the front porch. They took a seat in a pair of rocking chairs across from each other. It was a lovely night. The wind was still and the temperature barely seventy degrees.

"What's happening between us?" Danica heard herself asking. She just had to know. *Because I'm in love with you.*

"I'm not sure."

Honesty was very important right now because she had reached the point of no turning back. "What do you want to see happen?"

"You tell me, because the last time I checked you were engaged."

Damn, in all the excitement, she had forgotten about that. She stared over at him, trying to get her words together.

Jaden swung around on his chair. "I need to know if you're still planning to marry him."

God, how was she supposed to answer that one? "Well…yes."

She had not expected the look of disappointment on his face. Did her engagement really matter to him? Deep in her heart, she hoped it did. And if he gave her any indication he loved her, she would tell him it had all been one big lie. But right now she needed the false engagement to hide her true feelings.

"Just curious. You know I'm not looking for anything long term or a commitment," Jaden said quietly. "We both know we have no future. But until I get you out my system, I want to spend every moment I can with you."

"No commitments, no heartache, right?" she said.

He nodded. "Just pleasure."

She hesitated, then asked, "Don't you ever get tired of meaningless relationships? Don't you ever want to fall in love?" even though she already knew the answer.

Sighing, he answered, "I don't have room in my heart to love again. Right now I'm enjoying you being in my life."

Again. She gasped inwardly. Had he really loved her once? Please, God, don't tell me I made a mistake.

Jaden turned to her. "Come here." Danica rose and moved over and lowered herself onto his lap. "I'm crazy about you. I don't want anything to spoil the rest of our time together."

Their eyes met. Danica took a deep breath, and even though it wasn't what she wanted to hear, she agreed. "Okay."

Noticeably pleased, Jaden rose and carried her up to the master bedroom that was tastefully decorated in rich greens and gold and dominated by a king-size bed. Within minutes they were undressed and beneath his sheets, kissing, touching, feeling—she couldn't get enough.

Jaden's hand slid down between her legs and he nudged her thighs farther apart, then slid his fingers between her folds. Danica whimpered his name and lifted her hips, coaxing him farther, needing to feel him deep inside her. "Jaden," she sighed.

"Not yet, sweetheart," he whispered as his tongue trailed across her nipple, over her stomach to her belly button. "I want to take my time making love to you."

The husky whisper was music to her ears. *Making love.* Oh, how she wished it was so. That Jaden loved her the way she loved him, and that their time together never had to end.

Moving lower, he caressed the inside of her thigh with his lips, then drew his tongue to her sweet essence, where he licked hungrily and had her squirming and whimpering for more. Just when she didn't think she could take any more, his tongue moved to her hood, slipped underneath and suckled her clit gently.

"Jaden, yes!" she gasped as she tried to fight the intensity. But it was so good, she couldn't even focus. It was torture. Sweet sensual torture. *He's mine. All mine.* Even if it was only temporary, she would milk it for all it was worth. While he applied pressure to her slick center with his thumb, Jaden plunged his tongue inside her tender walls, and her hips jerked off the bed. "Yessss!" she cried as she rocked her hips against his mouth. It felt so good. No sooner had she come and her legs collapsed onto the bed then Jaden rolled on top of her and his lips came down on hers. The kiss became deeper and more passionate, and she wrapped her arms around him, taking everything he had to offer. Finally,

Jaden pushed her legs apart and handed her a condom from the nightstand, which she quickly rolled over him. Bracing one hand on either side of her head, he looked down at her as he plunged inside.

"Oooh!" she moaned, and then they found a rhythm and rode the storm together. She was his. Tonight. Tomorrow. Until he worked her out of his system, she belonged to him. And at the back of her mind she hoped that day would never come. When she finally came, her orgasm was so powerful she forgot to breathe, forgot everything except that Jaden was inside her and that she loved him.

Afterward, lying in a tangle of his sheets, Danica rested her head on his chest while he held her. Her heart skipped a beat, and she knew there would be a part of her that would be his for the rest of her life, even long after their relationship had ended.

"You're the first woman to stay in this house."

Her heart beat rapidly at the confession. What did that mean? "Why me?"

"Because you're special, Danica. And even though I'm not prepared to deal with what I feel when I'm with you, I'm in no rush for you or that feeling to go away."

Danica snuggled deeper. His words touched her, and she knew she would keep them close for a long time. Even after everything was said and done, his words and their memories would burn inside her.

Chapter 17

Danica, Sheyna and Brenna spent Saturday afternoon shopping down at Rehoboth Beach. Danica found a fantastic sale on designer sandals that she couldn't resist. Thank goodness for credit cards! Four hours had passed before their feet began to scream for the three of them to take a break. After going back and forth, they agreed on McCurry's Seafood House.

The hostess escorted them to a comfortable booth for four near the rear of the building next to a large picture window that showed off the harbor where sailboats lined the dock.

Danica took a sip of her water, then leaned back on the cushions with a heavy sigh.

Sheyna and Brenna looked at each other and shared a smile.

"Did we wear you out?" Brenna asked with a knowing look.

"You know you did. I've always been a shopper but never like that."

Sheyna smiled across the table. "That's because what we just did is called *bargain* shopping."

Brenna nodded with amusement. "Which means we spend hours searching racks looking for bargains. Finding one treasure makes it worth wasting half your day."

"We definitely found quite a few treasures."

"Yes. We did," Sheyna said and held out the tennis bracelet on her wrist. The price had been too good to resist. "My husband won't know until we get our credit card statement that he's already bought my birthday present."

Danica laughed. "What if he's already gotten you something?"

With the glass to her lips, Sheyna's eyes sparkled as she gazed over the rim of the glass. "Then I guess I'll have two."

The women shared a laugh. Danica loved the relationships her friends had with their husbands. Could she ever be so lucky?

While they studied their menus, she couldn't help but think about Jaden. The two weeks had been everything she could dream about in a relationship. It was as if they had turned back the clock nineteen months and everything was as it should be. She was now ready to talk about what happened to their relationship and see if maybe they could make things right again, but first she had to tell Jaden the truth. She wasn't engaged.

They each ordered a bowl of crab bisque and Mediterranean tilapia over couscous and golden raisins.

Danica noticed Sheyna giving her a funny look. "What's wrong?"

"Okay, I've been trying to be good and stay out of your business but I can't resist asking you a question a second longer."

"Why am I not surprised?" Brenna playfully pursed her lips and stared at her out the corner of her eye.

Sheyna playfully bumped her with her hip and they all shared another laugh.

"What would you like to know?" Danica asked with laughter still in her voice.

Sheyna leaned forward with her elbows resting on the table. "Do you love Jaden?"

"Yes," she confessed without hesitation.

"I knew it!" Brenna exclaimed.

Sheyna snorted rudely. "I never doubted it for a moment. So then, what is the problem?"

Danica had been keeping it to herself for too long. "Back when we first started dating, Jaden made a bet with his brother that he would have me eating out of the palm of his hand."

Brenna gave her a puzzled look. "Which brother?"

She shrugged. "He said big brother but I think he was talking to Jace."

Sheyna stirred her straw and snorted rudely. "I'm not surprised. My husband has this competitive edge about him that drives me crazy."

It was Brenna's turn to nudge her in the shoulder. "I don't see how. The two of you are just alike."

"Anyway…" Sheyna turned her attention back to Danica. "So that's why you lied and told Jaden you were engaged?"

Her eyes grew large with surprise. "You knew about that?"

"There isn't too much that gets past this family."

"I see."

Their waitress returned with their bisque. Sheyna waited until she was gone before continuing. "Jaden didn't tell us the details. All he said was that it was over, and that you were engaged to someone else. He tried to hide it but I could tell he was really hurt."

"And you don't think I was hurt finding out that he had made a bet as to how fast he could wrap me around his finger?" Danica said, and sounded angrier than she'd intended. The last thing she wanted was for them to know how much he hurt her.

Brenna pursed her lips. "I can't believe Jaden would do something like that. Are you sure you heard him right?"

"Positive." She took a sip of her soup even though she had suddenly lost her appetite. Maybe loving him again was not a smart thing to do.

"Are the two of you ready to try again?"

"I'm not sure," she began, then wiped her mouth with her napkin before continuing. "I love Jaden with all my heart, but there is no way I could set myself up for failure again."

"Has he told you he loves you?"

"No." And she doubted that he would. "Jaden proposed sex and nothing more." She wasn't naïve enough to think that things would be different this time even though in the back of her mind she wished they would. "I thought after I agreed to his proposal things would change."

Sheyna's brow rose. "And it hasn't?"

"No, our relationship is strictly sexual."

"But don't you want more?" Brenna asked.

"Yes, but since I can't deal with another heartbreak, what we have works out wonderfully."

Sheyna gave a rude snort. "I don't believe you."

"Well, believe it. Our relationship *is* strictly sexual." But even as she said that she knew she was lying. She was head over heels in love, and when their relationship finally ended she would have her heart broken once again.

"Proposal?" Brenna looked from one to the other with confusion. "Where did that idea come from?"

"Jaden's. He has this crazy idea that the only way for us to finally get each other out of our systems is to go for it and then both go our own separate ways," Danica said with ridicule.

Sheyna's eyes narrowed. "And is it working?"

"No."

The women laughed and discussed how clueless men could be at times.

Sheyna gazed across the table with a sly look. "What you need to do is turn the tables on him?"

"Like what?"

"It's time for Jaden to grow up. Show him what he's going to be missing. That's what I did to Jace."

Sheyna laughed while she told Danica how she showed up at his condo dressed in a French maid's uniform with a feather duster and stiletto heels. She had lost a bet and in turn had to wash his windows. By the time she left, she had the man eating out of the palm of her hands.

Danica's stomach hurt with laughter. As cool and confident Jace was, it was hard to imagine him off his game.

"This is a short-term relationship, right?" Sheyna asked, and Danica nodded. "Then if you really want Jaden you need to show him what he's losing."

Brenna nodded. "I'm not big on playing games like

my girl here is, but this is one time that I have to agree. Men sometimes need a little push. You're a beautiful woman. A swimsuit model. Just pretend you're walking down one of those runways and you'll have that man going crazy."

The more Danica thought about it, the more she liked the idea. If she wanted Jaden in her life, then she needed to do whatever she could to keep him there.

You're getting yourself in too deep.

Dumb move and Jaden knew it. The more time he spent with Danica, the more he wanted to be with her. It was crazy and he was starting to think that maybe he needed to go and see a shrink because something had to be mentally wrong with him. Danica was the one woman who had the ability to break his heart, and he knew that because she had already done it once. Now he was setting himself up for a possible second heart-break.

Tilting his can, he took a long frustrated drink and didn't stop until he ran out of air. It was crazy yet he was powerless. The attraction between them was stronger than ever and no matter how much time he spent with her, he couldn't seem to get enough of her. The whole reason for this proposal was to work Danica out of his system once and for all. Now he was starting to believe that it had all been a big waste of time because he wanted her now more than he ever had. All he was doing was setting himself up for a major letdown.

But she was so damn beautiful, smart and sexy as hell.

He strolled over to the window with his hands shoved in his pockets. All he'd done with his proposal was manage to torture himself. He didn't want to be attracted to her, but from the way his heart squeezed whenever he thought of her, he couldn't deny that he felt something close to what he had felt a little over a year and a half ago.

Now what?

At some point the game would have to end. He couldn't hold her car hostage forever, although if he could come up with a way to hold on to it for another six months he would milk it for all it was worth. However, Danica was a smart woman and at some point she was going to realize that it didn't take that long to fix a car. The problem was he just wasn't ready yet to say goodbye.

Was it because he still loved her?

No, what he was feeling had nothing whatsoever to do with love. Loving her got him nowhere but heartache and disappointment. But it's hard not to think about what-if when you're with a beautiful, smart woman with a wonderful personality and a sense of humor to match.

Danica had everything he'd ever wanted in a woman.

And yet that still hadn't been enough.

Now she was back and they were both still attracted to each other, but unfortunately he had no intention of doing anything about it. Nope. He had no intention of getting hurt a second time. He was only interested in sex, and plenty of it, until he got her out of his system once and for all.

He finished his beer with a scowl. Who was he trying to fool? He could never get her out of his system. In fact he wanted her at his house right now lying on her back with her legs spread wide, and he lying between them.

"Jaden?"

Realizing his brother was asking him something, he shook his head to clear his thoughts. "Yeah?"

"I thought I came over here so we could watch the game?"

He moved back over to the couch and flopped down on the seat. "What are you talking about? We are watching the game."

Jace gave him an amused look. "No, I'm watching the game while you're daydreaming. And it's not hard to guess who's been on your mind lately."

"Get off it. Danica and I are just friends."

"Did I say any names?" Jace said, laughing.

"No, but I know what you're thinking. We've buried our differences and have been spending time together. She's been a big help these past couple of weeks."

"I just bet she has."

Jaden frowned. "What's that supposed to mean?"

Jace raised his palms in surrender and gave an innocent shrug. "Hey, I'm just saying it like I see it."

"Well, you got it all wrong."

"Whatever, man." He turned back to the game. "You need to just face it. You're still crazy about her."

"Why, when it isn't true?"

"Yeah, keep telling yourself that," he chuckled. "Me and Jabarie already got a bet going. So make sure you propose before Labor Day. It's riding on five hundred dollars," he added, then moved down the hall to the bathroom, chuckling to himself.

Chapter 18

Jaden finished a tune-up and slammed down the hood on a classic Monte Carlo. He had been going at it nonstop for the last several hours. It was better than thinking about Danica and wondering what she was doing. He had tried calling her last night, and she still hadn't bothered to return his call. Through his brother he knew she had gone shopping with the girls, but he had no idea where she was last night. He would have driven by her house if that wouldn't have classified him as a stalker.

He moved over to the sink and contemplated dropping by her house on the way home, breaking down her door or demanding to be let in if he had to. He needed desperately to hold her in his arms. His heart started pitter-pattering. Shaking his head, he pushed aside the ridiculous thought. As he lathered his hands, he found he couldn't get her out of his mind. All he could think about was her smile. Her eyes. Her soft sighs when he slid inside her body. She was quickly getting under his skin, and he wasn't sure yet if he wanted to do anything about it. After all, he was almost done with her car and then it was back to the way it once was, which was probably for the best. As long as she was around, his heart was in jeopardy. Danica, with whom he shared a part of his past, was a woman he wanted to know everything there was to know about, and that wasn't such a good idea. They were ex-lovers having a sexual fling. He wanted her in his bed and didn't have to make any kind of emotional connection to her, but his soul warned him it was already too late and staying far away from her was the only way to escape any kind of emotional attachment. Only he was already so involved that staying away from her wasn't even an option.

Jaden slid beneath a Cavalier and had just started working on a brake line when he heard the door open and close. He glanced over and tried to see around an air pressure machine, and all he could see was a pair of black rhinestone stilettos and pink painted toes. His hand stilled. That couldn't possibly be Danica, he thought. He slid out from underneath and saw those mile-long legs that traveled up to a short white robe.

"Good evening, big boy," she greeted with a smirk. She moved over to the car and leaned back against the hood with her thighs slightly parted.

He rose. "I've been calling you."

"I know. But instead of returning your calls, I thought I'd come over."

And boy, was he glad she had!

Lifting her off the floor of the garage, he placed her on the hood of the car and moved between her parted thighs. While gazing down at her, he slipped his hand beneath her robe, skimmed his thumb between her legs and moved upward beneath the edge of her panties, dipping into the heat of her valley. Her hips began to rock ever so slowly against this touch; warmth and dampness seeped deep inside her.

Then he leaned down and licked the tips of her breasts through the cotton fabric of her bra, suckled her already erect nipples. Her back arched and her head fell to the side, a moan escaping from her throat. At the same time he buried his thumb deeper. Heat rushed from the tips of her breasts to coil low and deep from the pleasure of his touch.

Danica tucked her bottom lip under her front teeth and whimpered, hips lifting to coax him farther, needing to feel him deep inside her. "Please," she breathed, needing his fullness, the length of him inside her.

"Not this time, Danica." His tongue trailed down between her breasts over her stomach. "I'm going to take my time making love to you."

Make love. That was exactly what it was, because she loved Jaden. There was no denying what she felt. It was too incredible to ignore. Jaden lowered her panties from her hips, while kissing the inside of her thighs. The feeling was so amazing, she felt as if she might be dreaming. If so, she never wanted to wake up.

Jaden drew his tongue to the center of her, and within seconds he had her begging for more. Pushing open her legs with his hands on the inside of her thighs, he teased her clit with the lightly rough tip of his tongue. "But not until you tell me how badly you want me."

"Jaden, please." Her breath was shallow and breaking on tiny gasps. She adored this man. She loved the way he made her feel. Danica tried to maintain control, but the pleasure was too strong, too intense. She couldn't take any more of his sweet torture.

He eased his finger from within her, moved back inside, pushing deeper along her upper wall while drawing his tongue along her stomach. A moan escaped her lips, and he plunged two fingers deep inside her and held still. "Tell me what you want, Danica."

Her hips arched off the hood. She was helpless as he held her dangling from a hair short of climax. "I want…I need you so badly I can't think straight," she managed, gasping for air. She rocked her hips against his hand, circling, pushing, needing.

Jaden pushed her thighs farther apart, and she inhaled as he slid his erection deep into her core ever so slowly. Her begging body took him fully. "It's all yours, baby," he said, pressing even deeper inside. Jaden pulled his hips back, then reentered her, building her desire again with slow strokes. Seconds away from climax, he stopped.

"Where are you going?" she asked, sounding almost desperate.

"I want you on top." He brought her to her feet, then took her hand and led her to the small room in the back that held a full-size bed and a television he used when he didn't feel like going home. Jaden lowered himself onto the bed and Danica climbed on top and straddled him.

While his eyes were closed, Danica watched Jaden's face as she slowly eased herself down over his entire length, then paused a moment to enjoy the sensation of him being inside of her.

Jaden's eyes fluttered open and met hers with warmth and intensity. Placing his hands against her hips, he slowly began to move inside her while using her hips as leverage to glide in and out. She whimpered softly with each stroke. "Oh, that feels good."

"Look at me," he insisted when her eyelids threatened to close. As soon as their eyes locked, he continued. "You're mine."

I'm yours. At the moment, Jaden had control over her mind and body. He wouldn't let her break away from his gaze. He didn't allow her to control their rhythm. She didn't know how much longer she could hold on. Her legs trembled and need had built so high she was ready to explode.

"I'm getting ready to come," he moaned.

His words were all she needed to hear. She exploded with pleasure. "Yes!"

"Let it go," Jaden coaxed as he continued his slow thrusts. Slipping a finger between them, he stroked the aching nub of her clitoris. Her release went on and on until finally he came, as well.

As her breathing slowed, Danica gazed down at his face and saw everything she was feeling.

Did that mean Jaden loved her, as well? She lowered herself onto his chest and closed her eyes, praying that what she saw was indeed real.

"Danica, look at me."

She raised her head and stared down into the face of the man whom she would love forever.

"We need to talk."

Oh, no. The time had finally come. He had worked her out of his system. "What about?"

"Us."

She knew better than to hope. It would only bring her more heartache. She knew when he had offered her a proposal that it was only temporary. Now their time together was ending. What she was about to say was going to be the toughest thing she had ever done. But she had to end it before he did.

"Jaden, we both know there *is* no us. We had an agreement. We would enjoy each other until we worked each other out of our systems. Let's leave well enough alone." The last sentence she barely worked past the lump in her throat.

"What if I want more? What if I told you I love you?"

Her pulse raced. "Do you? You told me that once before. Why should I believe you now?"

"Yes, I do. I mean it this time. For real."

She wished that was possible, but they'd already been down this road once. "No, you don't, not really, and neither do I."

He stared up at her for a long time as if trying to read her mind. "Then I guess we have nothing else to talk about."

She forced back the smile, then rose and straddled his lap. "That's where you're wrong. I can think of a few things, but they require nothing but body language."

Chapter 19

"I'm so glad you came over to help me. I tried to get Jace to help me, but he finds every excuse to put it off."

Danica smiled at Sheyna as she stepped through the door. "I was more than happy to come and help." Sheyna signaled for Danica to follow her through the large two-story home.

Sheyna had called her and asked her if she didn't mind helping her address thank-you cards for the gifts she received from her housewarming party. Her boutique was all set to open next Friday, and she didn't have anything else to do other than sit around and go crazy thinking about Jaden.

It had been over a week since Jaden told her he loved her. She didn't believe it then and she definitely didn't believe it now. As a result, it put an uncomfortable strain on their relationship and they barely spent any significant time together. This morning, however, she had no choice but to call him. Her sink had backed up and to avoid paying the weekend rate for a plumber, she had called and asked for his help. He immediately agreed to come over and look at it and was still at her house when she left to come help Sheyna. Danica had been tempted to stick around but she got the feeling that he didn't want her around anyway.

As she reached the kitchen, she spotted a beautiful Irish setter running around the backyard with Jabarie and an adorable little boy playing Frisbee.

"Who's the little boy?" Danica asked.

"That's Chris, my neighbor's little boy. He's always over here when Red comes by."

"What a beautiful dog."

"Red belongs to my mother-in-law," Sheyna began as she gazed out the sliding door with a look of admiration. "My mother-in-law isn't the easiest woman in the world to get along with, but she does have a soft spot for animals. She rescued Red from the Humane Society."

"Mrs. Beaumont went to an animal shelter?" Danica asked with disbelief.

Nodding, Sheyna chuckled. "I know. It's hard to believe, but she donates money to them every year and makes it her business to personally see where every dime of her money is going. She was standing in the lobby talking to the director when a woman came in with Red and said she had given up on trying to train the stubborn animal. Apparently she had kids and the dog didn't get along with them."

Her brow rose. "She and Chris seemed to be getting along just fine."

Sheyna nodded in affirmation. "That's Jaden's work."

She gasped. "Jaden?"

"Apparently the brothers have always been good with dogs but Jaden is a regular Dr. Doolittle. My mother-in-law was getting ready to hire a trainer when Jaden stepped forward and said he would train her himself. My husband and Jace, who both tried and failed, thought he was crazy. Jaden was so confident he bet both them fools five hundred dollars he would have that redhead eating out the palm of his hands within a month."

Something in her mind triggered and Danica's knees buckled. She quickly moved over and took a chair. "What did you just say?"

"I said, he bet them…" Sheyna's voice trailed off as she suddenly put two and two together. "Oh, my goodness! The bet! You overheard his bet about Red and thought he was talking about you!" She started laughing.

Danica was so stunned she dropped her head to her hands and groaned. "What in the world have I done?" It had all been a big misunderstanding. Had she really lost the man of her dreams over a big misunderstanding?

"Sweetie, I don't mean to laugh, but it is a little funny."

Danica didn't see anything funny at all. "Oh, no! Sheyna, what have I done?"

Sheyna's face grew serious as she took a seat beside her. "There's still time to fix things."

"I don't think so. I told him there was nothing between us. I haven't even told him there was no fiancé."

Sheyna frowned. "You're kidding? I thought that was handled a long time ago."

"No. I didn't."

"I think you need to go see him and explain everything. He'll understand."

Danica finally looked up and flashed her a smile. "You're right and I plan to go and do just that after we get these cards done."

"Sound like a good plan."

Jaden had just finished fixing the leaking faucet when the phone started ringing again. Always one who respected another's privacy, he ignored it again. But what if it was Danica trying to call him? he wondered. The phone in the kitchen didn't offer caller ID.

This afternoon, on his way to Danica's house, he had changed into his work pants and had accidentally left his cell phone in his other jeans. So if she had tried calling that number, she wouldn't have had any luck.

For the last several days, he been doing everything in his power to stay away from Danica after admitting he loved her and having his words tossed back into his face…again.

For the last couple weeks he had fought anything developing between them that involved his heart. Yet while they made love at his garage, it finally hit him. Danica had stolen his heart and he found he was happy to give it to her. He no longer wanted to fight his feelings anymore. She consumed his mind, his every thought. Every evening he was anxious to rush into her arms. He could no longer fight those feelings. He no longer wanted to, and when Danica returned from Jace and Sheyna's, he planned to carry her off to bed and hold her there hostage until she took his confession seriously. He loved her and was not going away.

He reached for his toolbox and started packing up his tools. But by the time he put his pipe wrench away, the phone started ringing again. He finally reached for it. "Hello?"

"Hey, whassup? This is Kenyon. Is Danica there?"

Jaden was stunned into silence. Kenyon? Her fiancé was calling. What the hell was going on? "She's not here at the moment."

There was a long pause before the heavy voice on the other line asked, "Who are you?"

Jaden wanted so badly to tell him, "The brotha who's been sleeping with your fiancée for the last month," but he was a better man than that. "Jaden. A friend."

"Jaden, huh? I've heard her talk about you."

Really? He could just hear the two of them having a good laugh about him. "I've heard about you, as well. Congratulations on your engagement."

"Thanks, man. I hope I can get back in town in time to make my fiancée an honest woman."

Jaden's mind went on alert. "When are the two of you planning to get married?"

"This weekend."

Jaden felt as if someone had just stuck a knife in his heart.

"Well, can you tell Danica I love her and that I'll be arriving on Friday?"

Like hell he would. His competition was coming to town. He'd be damned before he made things easy for him. Yet he heard himself say, "Yeah, I'll tell her."

He hung up and felt as if a fist were in his chest squeezing his lungs. This couldn't be happening. Her fiancé was supposed to be a fake?

She never admitted that Kenyon was a fake.

That was true. He just assumed she was lying because his sister, Sheyna and Brenna had pretty much admitted that it was all a game. But they were wrong. Danica was really engaged and her fiancé was on his way back into town to marry her.

As soon as they finished addressing envelopes, Danica hopped into her car and hurried home. She had called Jaden but had gotten no answer. She had tried her house even though she knew he wouldn't answer her home phone. Anticipation raced up her spine. She needed to talk to him and let him know how wrong she was, but most of all she had to let him know she never stopped loving him.

She pulled into her driveway and spotted Jaden loading his truck and her heart soared with excitement. Quickly, she stopped her car and climbed out almost tripping over her heels and rushed over to him.

"Hey, baby," she said, then moved over and pressed her hand to his chest and kissed him, but instead of returning the kiss, he was stiff and unresponsive. "Is something wrong?"

"Nope, nothing's wrong," Jaden said as he moved away from her embrace and closed the back of his SUV. "Your plumbing is fixed and I should have your car ready tomorrow."

"My engine is ready?"

"Yes." He put the toolbox in the trunk. "I also decided to hire Martina."

She flinched. Jaden's words were like a slap in the face. "Martina? I thought *we'd* agreed she wasn't a good choice."

He simply shrugged. "I thought about it and think she's just what I need."

Danica dropped a hand to her hip with straight attitude. "What the hell is that supposed to mean?"

"It means that we had a deal. I needed to get you out of my system once and for all so that we could both move on with our lives."

Her pulse raced. "Are you saying that you are over me?"

"Yep."

Not again. "The other night you told me you loved me."

He rested a hip against his SUV and met her gaze head on. "I do love you and always will, but I'm not in love with you and that's a different story altogether."

"You're an asshole."

Jaden had the nerve to laugh. "I've been called worse. It's been fun but I think it's time for me to get back to business, and for you to focus on your future with your *fiancé*."

"But I'm—"

He waved his hand. "It doesn't matter. I hope we can be friends."

Danica closed her mouth. There was no point in telling him now that she wasn't engaged. It didn't seem to matter anyway. "Sure, maybe I'll even invite you to my wedding," she added sarcastically.

He turned and gave her a hard look, and she would have to be blind to have missed the jealousy lurking in the depths of his eyes. What was he jealous about? After all, he had broken her heart. Again.

Without making herself look any more foolish, she turned and headed into the house, leaving him standing there.

Danica kept walking to her bedroom, where she collapsed on her bed and started crying. It wasn't long before she heard his car pull away from the curb and down the street.

Jaden didn't really love her. After everything that had happened between them she had hoped that once she confessed the misunderstanding, everything in her world would be right again. Only she never got a chance to tell him because as far as he was concerned their agreement to each other had been fulfilled and their relationship was now over. Tears started streaming down her face. Danica was so angry she was tempted to pick up the phone and call his cell phone and cuss him out. But he didn't have his phone, so that would be a big waste of time. Never again would she put herself out there that way for a man to stomp on her heart. Because while being naïve, she had allowed Jaden to crush her heart twice.

The phone rang and she snatched it up hoping that it was him so she could give him a piece of her mind.

"Hello?"

"Danica, girl. You okay?"

She groaned at the sound of her big sister's voice. "I'm fine."

"You don't sound fine."

"That's because I put myself out there again and got crushed."

Maureen breathed a sigh of despair. "I guess that means things aren't working out with Jaden."

"Hardly. As far as he's concerned we had an agreement and it's done, so now it's time to move on."

"Ouch!"

Danica released a heavy sigh. "The worst part about it, Maureen, is it's all my fault. If I never ended our relationship none of this would have happened. He resents me for breaking his heart yet he's doing the same thing to me."

"Don't you dare take the blame! You had every reason to end that relationship after you overheard what he said about you."

"That's what I'm talking about. It was a big misunderstanding." She settled back on the bed and told her sister about Red and the five-hundred-dollar bet. As soon as she was finished Maureen exploded with laughter.

"You mean to tell me all this time he was talking about a stupid dog?"

"Yep."

She laughed some more.

"Just let me know when you're done," Danica said sarcastically.

"I'm sorry, sis, but that's the craziest thing I've ever heard."

Danica gave a weary sigh. "I know and now it's too late to fix things."

"It's never too late. Do you love him?"

"With all my heart."

"Then show him how much."

Danica thought about what her sister said. She didn't know if she could take rejection from him again.

"We're Dansforth women. I know you'll come up with a plan," Maureen said with confidence she didn't feel.

"I'm going to have to think about that one."

"Ooh!" Maureen cried in the phone. "I almost forgot the reason I called. Did Kenyon call you?"

"No, or at least I don't think so. I've been out all afternoon and there weren't any messages on the phone."

"He's coming home."

"What? When?"

"He's flying into Dover on Friday before he heads to Virginia. It appears he and Gloria decided not to wait until this fall and are going to get married while he's home."

"Oh, that's wonderful. I'm so happy for them."

"So am I. Anyway, I'll be flying in on Thursday, so I'm expecting you to pick me up in Baltimore."

"You know I will." She gave a dreamy smile. "My little brother's getting married."

"Yep, he beat you to the altar. Now we need to work on fixing your problem."

Danica grunted. "Jaden is going to have to make the next move. I'm tired of being the only one putting myself out there. If he really wants me, then he's going to have to show me himself."

"You can be so stubborn at times."

"I get it, honestly."

They shared a laugh and for the first time in the last thirty minutes she felt as though everything was going to be all right.

Chapter 20

Jaden tried to focus on changing the sparkplugs in a Chevy Impala, but he couldn't because Danica was still on his mind. Lying to her the other day was the hardest thing he had ever done. But he was angry, because coming this Saturday she was going to be marrying someone other than him. The thought of some other man making love to her the way he did made him sick to his stomach.

His gaze rested on the Cavalier. He would never be able to look at it without remembering making love to Danica. Even now he yearned to be deep inside her, and having her joined with him. That night had been a pivotal moment, one that had given him a sense of wholeness he'd never known was missing. It was also the night he admitted being in love with Danica and her throwing his confession back in his face. Angrily he reached for a monkey wrench and tightened his hold. All that time she had been saying no and denying him was because she had loved someone else. Hell, what right did he have to be mad? She had been honest from the start. She was engaged to marry someone else. That day had finally arrived. Tomorrow she would be walking down the aisle to marry someone else.

Jaden looked up to see his sister and Sheyna coming his way. Oh, boy, the two of them together spelled *trouble*.

"Hey, little bit."

"Don't little bit me," Bianca snapped. "What happened with you and Danica?"

"Nothing."

Sheyna stepped forward. "But I thought the two of you were getting back together?"

"I changed my mind."

Still shaking her head, Sheyna moved closer to point a finger at him. "You are too stubborn for your own good. I thought once she told you about overhearing your bet and thinking you were talking about her everything between the two of you would be okay?"

"Bet? What are you talking about?"

"That stupid bet you and Jace had about taming Red. Danica overheard you talking to Jace on the phone about wrapping that redhead around your finger and she thought you were talking about her."

"What? Why didn't she say anything?"

Bianca slugged him in the arm. "Why do you think? You broke her heart."

He turned angry eyes on her. "She's the one who is engaged. Not me."

Sheyna laughed. "I thought we'd already gone

through this. She isn't engaged. That was the excuse she came up with after overhearing you on the phone."

"I just talked to her fiancé on the phone."

They gave him a puzzled look.

"Kenyon. He's flying in today."

Sheyna and Bianca looked at each other and then started laughing.

"What the hell is so funny?"

"Kenyon is Danica's brother," Sheyna said between giggles. "He flew in today so he can marry his fiancée, Gloria."

"Her brother?"

"Jaden, I thought you were smarter than that." Sheyna started laughing harder. "Wait until I tell Jace this."

"Ha-ha! I answered her phone. He didn't mention anything about being her brother."

"He didn't have to. You just assumed that he wasn't."

"Come on, Bianca, I need to go and call my husband. Good job, Jaden."

"Yeah, good job," Bianca repeated.

Sheyna turned and stopped before moving though the door. "By the way, Danica won't be back until Monday."

They were still laughing as they moved out of the garage.

Danica returned home after a wonderful weekend and a beautiful wedding. She didn't think she had ever cried so much in her life. Most of her tears were of joy for her brother. The others were for her own pathetic life.

It was less than a week before her grand opening and all she could think about was Jaden. She didn't know why she bothered wasting any time thinking about the man, especially after the way he had treated her. Unfortunately, she couldn't blame anyone but herself. She knew when she had first agreed to his proposal that she was running the risk of heartbreak, yet she hadn't expected to hurt quite this much the second time around.

Danica unpacked her suitcase, then took a nice long shower. By the time she had dressed comfortably in a kimono and had moved into the kitchen to make herself a cup of tea, she was starting to feel a little better. Tomorrow Brenna, Sheyna and Bianca were coming over to the shop and, while they drank wine and listened to some old school jams, they were going to decorate the boutique for her grand opening on Friday. The excitement of finally opening for business brought a smile to her lips.

As soon as she removed her mug from the microwave she heard a knock at the door. Danica moved to the door and opened it. When she saw who was standing on the other side, she rolled her eyes, then turned away. "What do you want?"

Without waiting for an invitation, Jaden stepped inside. "To bring you the keys to your car and to talk."

She glanced out into her driveway and couldn't resist a smile at seeing the gleaming candy-apple-red beauty sitting outside. Jaden had cleaned her up beautifully. "Thank you," she said quietly as he handed her the key.

"Now I want to talk about us."

She dropped her eyelids briefly and shook her head. "I tried to do that the other day, only you refused to tell me what was bothering you."

"Your fiancé. That's what was bothering me," he barked.

"You know good and damn well I didn't have a fiancé. In fact you knew all along. Yet you were just playing another one of your games."

"Yes and no. When I realized you weren't wearing a ring I thought you were lying and was determined to get you to tell me the truth. But when I spoke to your brother over the phone, naturally I assumed he was the fiancé you claimed to have. "

"That's my brother."

"How was I to know that?"

"You should have asked."

"Like you should have asked me about this phone conversation you said you overheard."

She took a deep breath and didn't bother to respond, because he was right. She, too, had jumped to conclusions.

"Now I want to know. Why did you leave me?"

"You know why."

"No, I don't." He paused and ran a frustrated hand across his locks. "Everything was fine between us. I told you I loved you. You told me you loved me yet the next morning you made up some story about having a fiancé, then packed your bags and left. I deserve to know why."

"Because I thought you were playing me. I misunderstood."

"You left me because you thought it was all a game?"

She reached out to touch him, then realized that he had tensed up and wasn't at all receptive to the idea. "I overheard your phone conversation."

Confused, he shook his head. "What did I say?"

"You said, 'I told you I'd have that redhead eating out of the palm of my hand.'"

"I don't remember saying that, Danica, but if I did I was talking about my mother's dog, not you. Back then,

The Player's Proposal

the only thing I knew was that I loved you. I was prepared to spend the rest of my life with you. Do you know I went through hell after you left me?"

Despite her best attempt to fight tears, her eyes glistened with them. "If you loved me so much, then why didn't you come after me?"

"Because you didn't want me. Because you were planning to marry another man. How much rejection does a man have to endure?"

Her eyes glistened with tears. "I was so hurt. I really thought you were talking about me. I just found out you were talking about the dog."

He shook his head and she could tell he was clearly disappointed. "I loved you with everything I had."

"And I loved you, as well." *And I still do.* "I misunderstood just like you did about my brother."

"Without trust a relationship has nothing, and it's apparent that we don't trust each other enough."

"You're right."

"So where do we go from here?"

She shrugged. "I don't know but without trust things will never work between us."

"I agree. We also need love."

She flinched at the word and waited for him to tell her that he really loved her. If he did, she would jump in his arms and stay there forever.

"Do you love me, Danica?"

"Do you love me?"

He gave a nervous laugh. "Danica, this is not a competition. Either you love me or not."

"How do I know this isn't another one of your bets?" she replied defensively.

"Because it's not." Shaking his head, he gave another

nervous chuckle. "Listen, you just got back from your trip. You're tired and defensive. Maybe this isn't a good time to be having this discussion. Why don't we both take a few days and think?"

"Fine." Nodding, she moved over to the door and held it open. "Goodbye, Jaden."

He paused for a second, then nodded and with his shoulders back he walked out of her life. This time she was afraid it might be forever.

Chapter 21

Memorial Day weekend, Ujema Swimsuits officially opened for business. On Friday, the crowd arrived along with local media. Danica was so nervous she dashed off to the bathroom twice to empty her stomach. The cash register was ringing, and sales for the morning were a dream come true. She even signed a couple of autographs and gave beauty tips to several women.

According to the media, her boutique was one-stop shopping. Sunscreen, tanning lotion and sunglasses were at the counter. Flip-flops in all styles and colors on the shelves. Beach bags and towels to the right. Wraps and swimsuits to the left. She even had swimwear for men and children. Despite how miserable Danica was, she bubbled inside.

She was showing a customer to the dressing room

when the hairs at the nape of her neck started to tickle. She looked over near the menswear and there he was, Jaden. Her heart hammered against her chest. It had been four days since he'd ended their relationship and she hadn't heard a word from him. Wednesday Kyle had dropped by the boutique and she was pleased to hear that Jaden had sense enough to have hired Carrie Patrick to handle the front desk. She was going to do a fabulous job.

Danica helped the customer into the dressing area and when she came back, to her disappointment, Jaden was gone. It wasn't as though they had anything left to talk about. She loved him, but there was no way they could salvage what they'd had without trust. Too much had happened between them to fix things.

The rest of the afternoon passed and she was so busy with customers that she didn't have time to waste on Jaden. Nyree kept the register running while she moved around the boutique playing hostess and helping customers. If the crowd continued she would definitely be hiring another part-time salesclerk.

An hour before closing, Sheyna came into the boutique. "It doesn't look like things have slowed down at all," she said. She and Brenna had dropped by earlier in the afternoon.

"I know. Isn't it great?"

"Yes, definitely, but you've got to go out back. You'll never guess what's out there."

"What?"

"Go see," Sheyna urged, her eyes dancing with mystery as she gave her a gentle push.

Curious to see what had Sheyna all excited, Danica moved to the back door and stepped out into the alley behind the building and looked both ways, then frowned.

What in the world was Sheyna talking about? There wasn't anything out there but a Dumpster and boxes.

But before she could head back into the building, she heard movement. Someone ran up behind her, applied pressure to the side of her neck and then everything went black.

When Danica finally woke up the first thing she noticed was she was lying across a bed that wasn't hers. The next thing she noticed was Jaden sitting at the end wearing faded blue jeans and a white tank top.

"Where am I?"

"On board *Beaumont Beauty*."

She took a moment to clear the haze and tried to pinpoint the last thing she remembered and came up empty. "What am I doing on your father's yacht?"

"I brought you here so that we could be alone."

She closed her eyes briefly and slowly remembered Sheyna telling her to go out back to see something and then everything went black. Her eyelids fluttered open. "What did you do to me?"

Jaden's eyes sparkled knowingly. "It's a tactical move I learned while in the military."

"So you knocked me unconscious and whisked me off on your father's yacht to the middle of the ocean. That's kidnapping!"

A smile tickled his lips. "If you want to look at it that way. I call it a brotha doing what a brotha gotta do."

Danica wasn't the least bit amused. She sat up straight. "Why?"

His expression grew serious. "Because we needed to

talk without any distractions. I know with the boutique just opening that might take a few more days and we've both waited long enough."

Danica sprang from the bed. "Oh, no! The boutique! Who's—"

Jaden took her hand and pulled her back down onto the bed. "Relax. Nyree and Sheyna have things under control."

Exhaling, she allowed herself to relax a little. He was right. Nyree had been managing retail stores for years and was more than capable of handling things. Sheyna on the other hand…

"Sheyna helped you, didn't she?"

"Only after a lot of begging and a promise to be the godfather to her firstborn."

Danica should be mad at her good friend, but knew the matchmaker had only been trying to help.

Jaden shifted so he was facing her and took her hands in his. Heaven, how she missed his touch.

"Danica, I want to start by saying I'm sorry."

"For what?"

"For failing us. For not coming after you months ago and fighting for what we had." He took her hand and pulled her over onto his lap, then cradled her in the circle of his arms. "Danica, I loved you with everything I had and I should have fought for our love. Can you ever forgive me?" His voice was low and sensual.

Tears pushed to the surface of her eyes.

"I should be asking you if you'd forgive me. I heard you talking on the phone and I just assumed you were talking about me."

"What you should have done was cuss me out," he suggested with a playful grin.

"I should have but I was just so hurt and felt so betrayed. I had to do something to turn the tables on you."

"You definitely did that. Can I ask you where you came up with that idea of faking a fiancé?"

Danica dropped her eyes and smiled. "I saw it in a movie."

"Well, it worked." He squeezed her close, and she felt his warm lips against her forehead. "Woman, do you know how crazy you make me?"

"No, but maybe next time you won't wait so long to come after me."

"Uh-uh, there won't be no next time." She looked up and his face had grown serious. "From this point on we've got to promise each other that no matter what we'll talk before jumping to conclusions."

"Agreed." Leaning forward he met her lips with a warm, searing kiss, then pulled back.

She gazed up into his eyes and asked, "So now what?"

"Danica, when I walked into your boutique and saw you standing there, I realized I never stopped loving you. Since the day at the garage, I've needed to be near you." The heat of his body closed in on her, his words were soft and warm. He slid his hand along her back, then took her bottom in his hand and squeezed, angling her hips to press against him. "Right now I'm dying to be inside you. Do you know why?"

Danica bit her lip to keep from crying and shook her head.

Jaden slid his other hand beneath her blouse, tickled up her side, simmered over her breast and stopped over the beat of her heart. Sensations tingled in the wake of his touch. Her nipples budded, warmth stirred to swirls of heat. It was so hard for her to think when Jaden touched her, so difficult to breathe.

"Because I love you and there is no way I'm letting stubborn pride cause me to lose another year, another second without you in my life." His words were moist and warm against her mouth. "You drive me crazy when I'm near you, drive me insane when we're apart."

His words played in her heart and mind.

She focused on his handsome face. "I love you, too, but don't you dare do anything like this again!" she scolded. "I can't believe you kidnapped me in the middle of my grand opening."

"I had to make you believe that I love you," he said, his eyes darkening as he stared deep into her eyes.

"I believe you, because I also love you," she whispered, the words catching on her soul.

"Can you say that again?"

"I said I love you, Jaden. I never stopped loving you."

He laid her back onto the bed and they stripped away each other's clothing. As they came together in an orgasm more powerful than any before, words of love flowed again and again. Afterward, lying in a tangle on the bed Jaden brought his mouth down to her. "I doubt there'll be a dull moment in our bed for the next fifty years or so."

She smiled and snuggled closer to him. "You sure you'll be still operating properly at seventy-seven?"

"Sweetheart, I could be ninety but as long as you're around I'll never have a problem *rising* to the occasion."

Danica chuckled. "You better not, Jaden Beaumont."

"Never, Mrs. Beaumont."

She gasped and sat up in the bed, studying his eyes. "Did you just call me…"

"Yes, I am asking you to be my wife and the mother

of my children." He kissed her. "Danica, will you marry me?"

Tears filled her eyes. "Yes, Jaden. Yes. I'll marry you."

He kissed her once more, then sprang from the bed and reached for the phone on the wall.

"Who are you calling?"

"Jace."

"For what?"

"To let him know he won the bet."

"Bet?" she cried, then jumped from the bed and wrestled him for the phone. By the time they got through laughing, they made love again and hours later dialed the phone number together.

This was one bet where everyone came out a winner.

DON'T MISS
THIS SEXY NEW SERIES
FROM KIMANI ROMANCE!

THE BRADDOCKS

SECRET SON

*Power, passion and politics
are all in the family.*

HER LOVER'S LEGACY by Adrianne Byrd
August 2008

**SEX AND THE SINGLE BRADDOCK
by Robyn Amos**
September 2008

SECOND CHANCE, BABY by A.C. Arthur
October 2008

**THE OBJECT OF HIS PROTECTION
by Brenda Jackson**
November 2008

KIMANI™
ROMANCE

www.kimanipress.com

She faced the challenge of her career…

Seducing
the matchmaker

elaine overton

Acquiring world-renowned architect Derrick Brandt as
a client is a real coup for Noelle Brown's matchmaking
service. Finding him a mate will be no picnic, but as
attraction sizzles between them, they wonder if *their*
relationship could be the perfect match.

"Elaine Overton does a wonderful job conveying her
characters' feelings, their emotional baggage and their
struggles."
—*Romantic Times BOOKreviews*
on *His Holiday Bride*

*Available the first week of November
wherever books are sold.*

KIMANI™
ROMANCE

She was a knockout!

Love**TKO**

pamela yaye

Boxer Rashawn Bishop woos stunning
Yasmin Ohaji with finesse and fancy footwork,
and finally TKO's her resistance. But love means
making choices, and with his career on the line,
will he follow the lure of boxing…or the woman
he can't live without?

"A fun and lighthearted story."
—*Romantic Times BOOKreviews*
on Pamela Yaye's *Other People's Business*

*Available the first week of November
wherever books are sold.*

**Breaking up is hard to do…
even when you know it's right.**

NATIONAL BESTSELLING AUTHOR

*marcia
King-
Gamble*

first crush

Hudson Godfrey's new wine-making business leaves
him with no time for a relationship, so he breaks up with
one-of-a-kind woman Laila Stewart. Of course, he didn't
realize she would wind up moving to Washington state
and working with him. Or that their heated daytime
glances would lead to sizzling passionate nights. Now
he's starting to wonder if letting this alluring woman go
was the biggest mistake of his life….

*Coming the first wefi of November 2008,
wherever books are sold.*

ARABESQUE®

www.kimanipress.com   KPMKG1131108

"A delightful book romance lovers will enjoy."
—*Romantic Times BOOKreviews*
on *Love Me or Leave Me*

ESSENCE BESTSELLING AUTHOR

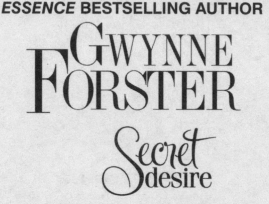

GWYNNE FORSTER

Secret desire

Their lives spared but nerves shattered in a
harrowing robbery, independent widow
Kate Middleton and her young son are rescued
by Luke Hickson, a handsome police captain still
reeling from a calamity of his own. Neither Kate nor
Luke expects, much less welcomes, their instant
attraction. But when trouble strikes again, Kate
realizes there's only one place she feels safe—
in Luke's strong embrace.

*Coming the first wefi of November 2008,
wherever books are sold.*

ARABESQUE®

www.kimanipress.com   KPGFI141108

ESSENCE BESTSELLING AUTHOR

DONNA HILL

Temptation

Liaisons, Noelle Maxwell's chic romantic retreat, is the ultimate fantasy. But there is no idyllic escape from her past, and Noelle has vowed to uncover the truth behind the mysterious death of her husband. Yet the only man she can trust is a stranger whose explosive sexuality awakens desire—and fear. Because Cole Richards has a secret, too....

"Riveting and poignant, this novel will transport readers to new heights of literary excellence."
**—*Romantic Times BOOKreviews*
on *Temptation***

Coming the first week of October wherever books are sold.

ARABESQUE®

www.kimanipress.com

NATIONAL BESTSELLING AUTHOR

ROCHELLE ALERS

invites you to meet the Whitfields of New York....

Tessa, Faith and Simone Whitfield know all about coordinating
other people's weddings, and not so much about arranging
their own love lives. But in the space of one unforgettable year,
all three will meet intriguing men who just might bring them their
very own happily ever after....

Long Time Coming

June 2008

The Sweetest Temptation

July 2008

Taken by Storm

August 2008

ARABESQUE®

www.kimanipress.com